# IN THE SHADOW
# OF THE TOWER

Books by

CAROLYN KEENE

*Nancy Drew Mystery Stories*

*Dana Girls Mystery Stories*

*The* DANA GIRLS *Mystery Stories*

---

# IN THE SHADOW
## OF THE
## TOWER

By

CAROLYN KEENE

---

Grosset & Dunlap, *Publishers*
**NEW YORK**

# CONTENTS

"Quiet!" said Louise. "We'll hide in the cave."

In the Shadow of the Tower

"Quick!" said Louise. "We'll hide in the cave."

*In the Shadow of the Tower*

# CHAPTER I

## The Lost Letter

"JEAN, I believe someone is following us!"

"Following us, Louise? What makes you think so?"

"Can't you hear the whistling?"

Jean and Louise Dana, two pretty sophomores at the Starhurst School for Girls, halted on the trail which led through the woods. It was early winter, and the ground was covered with snow. The bare branches of the frost-laden trees glistened in the sunlight.

"Listen!" said Louise. "I can hear it again."

On the still December air floated the notes of a plaintive whistling in a minor strain. It was not the warbling of a bird, nor did it seem like that of a human being. Puzzled, the girls looked behind them. There was no one in sight. The trail was deserted.

"It doesn't sound human," said Jean Dana,

1

"yet it *must* be. There's a sort of tune to it."

Suddenly the whistling ceased. In the distance the girls could hear the snapping of twigs. It was late afternoon. Jean and Louise had been skating on Mohawk Lake in the hills not far from Starhurst, and had left before their companions. They were not disposed to be frightened, but the strange whistling really mystified them.

"There *is* someone coming," insisted Louise. "Let's hide."

"Perhaps it's some of the other girls trying to scare us."

"Well, then, we'll just fool them."

The girls were near the outskirts of the woods where the trail dropped steeply down the hillside toward the meadows and the road below. They were familiar with the place, and knew that the path led past a natural cavern in the rocks not far ahead of them.

"Quick!" said Louise. "We'll hide in the cave."

The girls hurriedly descended the trail. The mournful and mysterious whistling was suddenly resumed, and they could still hear it when they reached the grotto. It continued as they scrambled into the gloomy hiding place among the rocks, where they crouched, watching the snow-covered path a few yards ahead of them.

In a short time they again heard the crackling of twigs, followed by the soft shuffling of footsteps in the snow. Jean clutched her sister's arm in excitement as a strange-looking figure suddenly came into view.

It was that of a boy—a slender youth with a pinched, white face. The girls judged him to be about nineteen years of age. He was a furtive, odd-looking creature in ragged clothes that looked as if they had been made for someone else. As he shuffled along the trail, he looked fearfully from side to side.

"Why, he's a hunchback," whispered Jean.

The poor boy was, indeed, deformed by a hump that distorted his back, giving him a grotesque and dwarfed appearance. He walked in an ungainly manner, one hand thrust inside his tattered coat.

As the girls watched tensely, the hunchback came to a halt, looked back down the trail, and then nodded his head in satisfaction.

"I'm safe here," he muttered. "There's no one in sight."

With that he sat down on a rock not far from the mouth of the cave. Rummaging in his pockets, he drew forth a long envelope, from which he extracted a letter.

The Dana girls regretted that they had concealed themselves in the cave. They knew they had nothing to fear from this pathetic cripple, and they had no intention of spying on him. However, not wishing to frighten the boy, they thought it best to remain where they were.

The letter, much-thumbed and frayed, appeared to be some kind of a legal document. The cripple read it carefully, muttering to himself in an undertone, while his thin face twitched strangely. Then, to the astonishment of the Dana girls, he began to cry.

It was evident that the letter had affected him deeply. The onlookers accordingly grew curious. They wondered what sort of message the document contained. Yet at the same time they were uncomfortable in the realization that they were peering at the secrets of a stranger.

"We ought to leave," whispered Jean.

Louise, however, cautioned her to stay.

"We can't go now. We'll only frighten the poor fellow."

Suddenly in the distance the girls could hear voices and shouts of laughter. The other students from Starhurst were sauntering down the trail from the lake.

The cripple scrambled hastily to his feet and cast a frightened glance back up the snow-covered path.

"Someone coming!" gasped the hunchback. "I can't let them find me."

In evident terror he ran ahead a few paces, then paused in indecision and finally turned back. He saw the gloomy mouth of the cave, plunged through the snow toward it, and crouched down among the rocks at the entrance. He had not yet seen Jean and Louise, as they had withdrawn to the deeper shadows of the cave and had there hidden themselves, scarcely daring to breathe.

Suddenly nearby them the high, harsh laugh of a girl rang out.

"Oh, it will be the joke of the term! First of all we'll leave a phone message for the Dana girls that their Uncle Ned is at the Continental House, and that they're to go to see him at once. Then we'll call up the clerk at the hotel and tell him that if two girls ask for their Uncle Ned Dana, they're to be sent to the State Hotel. We'll have them running all over Penfield looking for their precious relative, and when they get back to school they'll surely be late. Won't Mrs. Crandall give them a scolding?"

"Oh, Lettie," came a shrill giggle, "that's the best joke I've ever heard. We'll get even with them for a few things they've done to us."

Louise and Jean were very interested in the conversation which they had just overheard. The two persons sauntering down the trail were Lettie Briggs and Ina Mason, the only pupils at Starhurst with whom the Dana girls were not on good terms. Lettie Briggs, an

angular, snobbish individual, fond of impress
ing upon everyone the fact that she was the
wealthiest girl at Starhurst, was a very unpopular student because of her arrogance. Her
one and only friend, Ina Mason, was a meek,
toadying creature who seemed delighted to have
the rich Miss Briggs deign to notice her.

The pair had clashed with the Dana girls on
several occasions, for Lettie and Ina had a
habit of playing mean practical jokes, and
nothing delighted Jean and Louise more than
to score a point against the unpopular chums.

Louise almost laughed aloud. She knew that
she and Jean had overheard the details of an
elaborate joke which was to be played upon
them. Forewarned was to be forearmed. The
sisters heard nothing further of Lettie's plan,
for Ina Mason said quickly:

"We'll talk it over when we get back to
school. The others are coming."

In a few minutes a laughing, chattering
group of girls came down the trail and passed
the cave, unaware of the hidden watchers.
Jean and Louise had a fleeting glimpse of gaily-
colored sweaters and scarfs as their schoolmates passed by. Then the clamor of voices
died away as the students descended the hillside.

The hunchback, who had been crouching near
the mouth of the cave, rose to his feet. He

groped in his pocket, withdrew the letter, and began to study it once more.

"We can't stay here," whispered Jean. "And I'm cold. I'm going to speak to that poor boy."

Louise advanced quietly toward the opening of the shallow cavern.

"We're very sorry," she said apologetically. "We aren't spying on you, but——"

There was a cry of alarm as the cripple wheeled about and stared at them. Then he turned and fled as though terrified. Tripping and stumbling among the snow-covered rocks, he ran from the trail directly toward the edge of a steep cliff that dropped to the meadow below.

"Come back!" cried Jean. "You'll fall!"

The lad paid no attention to her warning. In his mad flight he scrambled desperately to the very brink of the cliff. The girls gasped, as he suddenly slipped on the ice, staggered and fell. The letter flew from his hand.

The white sheet of paper, together with a green object that had been concealed in its folds, was whisked up by the breeze. The two articles fluttered over the rocks and went sailing out toward a distant field.

Jean and Louise hastily ran to the assistance of the hunchback, who lay panting and gasping in the snow.

"Are you hurt?" asked Louise. "We didn't mean to frighten you."

The cripple thrust the proffered hand aside. "My money! My letter!"

The girls knew then that the green object had been a bill.

"We'll help you get your money again," said Jean. "Look! It has blown down into the field."

The letter and the greenback had come to rest in the branches of a clump of bushes not far from the base of the cliff. But even as she spoke, the wind suddenly dislodged the letter and the bill from the trees and sent them both skimming across the snow.

"I must have it back," declared the hunchback fearfully. "It's all the money I have in the world——"

Then Jean uttered a cry of dismay. From among the rocks there emerged a lean black animal with a bushy tail—a fox. The little beast leaped playfully at the fluttering papers, snapped up the greenback, then sprang lightly toward the letter. A gust of wind sent it flying out of reach. The little beast whirled in pursuit, jumped into the air, and deftly caught the swirling bit of paper.

Then, like a fleeting black shadow against the white snow, the fox raced away across the meadow.

# CHAPTER II

## Josy Sykes

THE Dana girls were overcome with concern. They felt that they were somewhat to blame for the loss of the letter and the money.

Sobbing with grief, the cripple was already hastening down the trail, wailing:

"Oh, the fox is gone. Gone with my letter."

As the animal scurried off across the meadow, Jean and Louise scrambled down the hillside.

"We'll never catch it!" gasped the younger Dana girl.

"But we may find its den," replied Louise.

When they reached the foot of the trail, the cripple was already following the tracks across the snow. The sly fox, however, had disappeared. The girls traced the footprints as far as the meadow fence, but soon saw that the chase was futile.

It was growing dark, and the wind was rising. The breeze sent the snow shifting over the surface of the field, and the tracks were being blotted out swiftly.

The boy sank down beside the fence and

burst into tears. Something about that heart-broken sobbing caught Jean's attention. She looked significantly at her sister. Louise uttered an exclamation of surprise.

"Why, he isn't a boy at all!" she cried.

"No boy ever cried like that," declared Jean.

The hunchback looked up, eyes filled with tears.

"No," the cripple sobbed, "I'm n-not a boy. I'm a g-girl. Oh, why didn't you leave me alone? I've lost my letter and my money, and now I don't know what to do."

Jean sat down and slipped an arm around the shoulders of the weeping girl.

"We're dreadfully sorry," she said, "but you mustn't blame us. We didn't intend to frighten you. We'll do everything we can to help you find your letter again."

"Indeed we will," Louise assured her. "Was it important? Was there very much money?"

It was in her mind that she and Jean might make good the loss if the amount were small.

"It was all the money I had," confessed the girl in the snow. She was a little calmer now. "It was *a thousand-dollar bill!*"

The Dana girls were stunned by this unlooked for statement.

"A thousand dollars?" exclaimed Jean incredulously. "In one bill?"

The two sisters at once scented a mystery. Those of our readers who have made the acquaintance of Louise and Jean in previous volumes of this series can readily understand that a problem of this kind would appeal to them. They possessed marked talent as amateur detectives, and had already been successful in solving two strange cases that had created a great deal of excitement and bewilderment at Starhurst.

In the first book which introduced the Dana girls, *By the Light of the Study Lamp,* they encountered many thrilling adventures in getting to the bottom of the mystery surrounding the theft of a study lamp given to them by their Uncle Ned. Their clever work in this affair had brought about the recovery of a fortune in jewels.

Jean and Louise were orphans. Louise, a pretty, dark-haired girl of seventeen, was rather quiet, and the more serious of the two. Jean, a year her junior, was fair-haired, boyish, and impetuous. They made their home with their uncle, Captain Ned Dana, who lived at Oak Falls, which was not far from Starhurst. He was skipper of the *Balaska,* one of the great trans-Atlantic liners. Aunt Harriet, his maiden sister, was housekeeper of the picturesque old residence on the outskirts of the town.

In the second volume of the series, *The Se-*

*cret at Lone Tree Cottage,* the Dana girls again proved their abilities as detectives when they solved the mystery surrounding the disappearance of Miss Tisdale, their young and beloved English instructress at Starhurst. In clearing up the case they also succeeded in restoring to a fine family a long-lost relative.

The success of the two sisters in these cases had given a decided impetus to their interest in detective work. It was only natural, therefore, that they should be excited by the mystery presented by the girl in boys' clothing, who had lost a thousand-dollar bill.

"I'm afraid we'll never find the money tonight," said Louise kindly. "It's getting dark."

The cripple agreed that further search was useless at the time.

"I'm going to stay in Penfield tonight," she said, "but I'll come back here early tomorrow and look for my money."

"We'll help you," Jean offered. "If we can find the den of that fox, we ought to be able to locate the money and the letter, too."

"Why," asked Louise, "are you dressed as a boy?"

A shadow crossed the thin face of the hunchback as she started to walk across the meadow.

"It's because I have run away."

At first she was not inclined to explain any-

thing further, but as they went back toward
the main road that led to Penfield the Dana
girls were so kind and sympathetic toward her
that she soon realized they were sincerely eager
to help her. At last, won over by their tact
and understanding, the hunchback told them
more of her story.

"My name is Josephine Sykes," she said.
"Everyone calls me Josy. I ran away from
the Home for Crippled Children at Bonny
Lake."

"Didn't they treat you well?" asked Jean.

"Well enough," replied Josy Sykes, with a
pathetic smile, "compared to the other places."

"What other places?"

"The farmhouses. Ever since I was fifteen
I have done housework on farms. Being a
cripple, I was never sent to any of the better
places. You see, I was left at the Home when
I was a baby."

"Oh!" exclaimed Louise. "Your father and
mother——"

"Dead," replied the girl shortly. "I don't
know anything about my folks. My uncle left
me at the Home. That's how I got my name.
He was Joseph Sykes and I was named after
him. I was brought up at the Home as a sort
of charity girl, because my uncle just seemed
to drop out of sight after he left me there.
I didn't mind going out to work at the farm-

houses, because I wanted to repay the people at the institution in some way, and it was time I was earning my own living anyway—but—oh, some of the places were *awful!* I ran away from the last one.''

Although Josy Sykes told her story in a matter-of-fact tone, the Dana girls sensed the tragedy of loneliness that had shadowed the life of the crippled girl. Yet they were still puzzled by her present disguise.

''Where did you go when you ran away from the farm?'' asked Louise.

''I went back to the Home. They were very kind to me—they have always been kind—and gave me a job in the office. I thought my bad luck was over, but it wasn't. I hadn't worked there two days before a big sum of money disappeared from the safe. There had been a benefit for the Home and the cash proceeds had come to nearly a thousand dollars. Every cent of it was stolen.''

''They surely didn't accuse you, did they?'' asked Jean indignantly.

The hunchback nodded.

''They thought I took it. You see, while I was away from the institution, an important letter came to the Home addressed to me. The secretary put it in the safe. She was on a vacation when I came back, and I suppose the superintendent forgot to tell me about my mail.

At any rate, I found the letter when I was putting some papers into the safe and naturally I took it. That was the one I was reading a little while ago. It was from my uncle, Joseph Sykes. He had enclosed a thousand-dollar bill. So you see, when I was accused of taking the benefit money from the safe, I was afraid they would find my thousand dollars——''

"So you ran away!" exclaimed Louise.

"I borrowed an old suit of clothes from a boy at the Home and climbed out of the dormitory window last night. I've been wandering about ever since."

The girls were deeply concerned over the plight of the unfortunate girl.

"What are you going to do?" asked Jean.

"I don't know," confessed Josy, her lips trembling. "I felt safe enough when I had the money—but now that it's gone—I haven't any money—I haven't any friends——''

Her voice faltered. With a cuff of her ragged sleeve she brushed away tears from her eyes.

"You have friends," Louise assured her. "We're your friends. You're coming to Starhurst with us, and we'll get some proper clothes for you. Then we'll talk to Mrs. Crandall. She is the headmistress at the school and perhaps she'll be able to help you."

Josy Sykes looked at the Dana girls gratefully.

"You're the very first strangers," she said, "who ever paid any attention to me or tried to do anything for me."

By this time they had reached the Penfield road. When they came within sight of Starhurst School, the Dana girls realized that their new acquaintance presented a grotesque appearance. Josy Sykes, who was evidently sensitive about her deformity, was conscious of her shabby clothes and bedraggled appearance.

"I—I can't go into that grand place with you," she said. "They'll all stare at me. People always do. Perhaps you had better leave me. I'll get along somehow."

"Nonsense!" said Jean warmly. "We're not ashamed of you."

As they approached the walk that led to the front entrance of Starhurst, they saw Lettie Briggs and Ina Mason standing on the pavement watching them in open-mouthed wonder. They heard a harsh cackle of laughter from Lettie, and then her high-pitched, disagreeable voice:

"Look what the Danas have picked up. They've been slumming."

A deep flush suffused Josy Sykes's pinched face.

"I don't like those girls," she whispered.

"They're laughing at me. I'm not going in with you."

Before the Dana girls could prevent her, she left the sidewalk abruptly and stepped out into the road. Confused by the rude stares and contemptuous laughter of Lettie and Ina, she failed to see a roadster which at that moment swept around a bend. She stepped directly into the path of the speeding car.

Jean screamed.

"Come back!" cried Louise.

Josy Sykes turned, saw the approaching machine, and uttered a shriek of alarm. She seemed frozen with fear. The man at the wheel of the roadster applied his brakes, but it was evident that he would be unable to bring the car to a stop in time. Josy Sykes wavered, moved as if to run back toward the curb, and then to the horror of the Dana girls she slipped on the icy pavement and sprawled helplessly in front of the oncoming wheels.

## CHAPTER III

### THE SHADOW

JEAN DANA did not hesitate. She sprang from the curb and grabbed Josy Sykes by the arm. Even as the driver of the car swung desperately to one side, Jean dragged the helpless girl out of danger.

The roadster flashed past, brakes screeching, and skidded to a stop. It had missed the cripple by a couple of inches.

The Dana girls helped Josy to her feet.

"Are you hurt?" demanded Jean anxiously.

Josy's face was white as she realized the narrowness of her escape.

"No," she panted. "And you saved my life!" she declared gratefully. "I should have been run down if you hadn't caught my arm in time."

The driver of the car, a stout, red-faced man, was stepping from his machine.

"Close call!" he said. "A mighty narrow squeak. Young lady," he remarked to Jean, "if you had been half a second slower, I'd be reporting a serious accident to the police."

Some of the Starhurst girls were already

running toward the scene. Jean took Josy
Sykes by the arm.

"Come!" she said. "Let's hurry into the
school."

The little hunchback was embarrassed with
the thought of being the central figure of any
excitement, so before the gathering crowd
could learn what had happened, the Dana girls
and Josy were hustling up the school steps.
They reached the study unobserved, and there
Jean and Louise quickly found a complete out-
fit of clothing for their new acquaintance.
Within half an hour the ungainly crippled boy
of the hillside had vanished, being transformed
into a shy, wide-eyed girl in a neat blue woolen
dress. Josy's gratitude was pathetic.

"It's a long time since I've worn silk stock-
ings," she sighed luxuriously, looking at her
slender ankles. "You are too good to me."

Josy was a little more cheerful as they went
down the stairs, although she was still pain-
fully conscious of her deformity and shrank
from the curious glances of the students whom
they encountered in the hall. When she
reached Mrs. Crandall's office, however, she
was immediately put at her ease by the kindly
manner of the headmistress. The Dana girls
told their story, and the mentor of Starhurst
School was at once sympathetic.

"If you are looking for work, Josy," she

told the hunchback, "I can offer you a tempo-
rary position in the linen room. It will give
you time to look around and make plans for
the future."

There were tears of happiness in the cripple's eyes.

"It's wonderful of you to give me this
chance," she said. "I promise to work hard
and try to please you."

"I'm sure you will," said Mrs. Crandall.
"And I sincerely hope you will find your
money. If you wish, you may take time off tomorrow afternoon to go back and look for it."

"Exactly what we were going to ask, Mrs.
Crandall," said Jean promptly.

The headmistress smiled.

"I thought so." She turned to Josy. "Was
the letter very important?"

The cripple hesitated.

"Yes," she said simply. "It was important."

Josy said nothing more about the missive.
When she returned to the study with the Dana
girls, they noticed that she was evasive and
silent whenever the letter or the robbery at the
Home for Crippled Children was mentioned.

After dinner the girls left Josy in the room
in the servants' wing to which she had been
assigned by Mrs. Crandall. Louise was puzzled
by the girl's reticence about her private affairs.

"Do you think she *could* have stolen that money?" she said to Jean.

"I don't believe Josy Sykes would take a nickel that didn't belong to her."

"It would be dreadful if the police were to come here and take her away. After all, Jean, her story is very strange. She tells us she received a thousand-dollar bill in a letter, but she hasn't said anything more than that. Who sent her that much money? And why?"

"Suspicious?" asked Jean.

"Well, after all, we don't know anything about Josy."

"I know what we'll do. We'll call up the Home for Crippled Children and ask about her," Jean decided promptly.

Over the telephone the superintendent of the institution was gruff.

"We once had a girl here by that name," he said, "but she isn't here any more. Are you a friend of hers?"

"Well—yes," admitted Louise.

"If you hear from her," said the superintendent, "I wish you would let us know. We're very eager to find Josy. Something very unpleasant happened here just before she left. A big sum of money was taken from the office safe, and we'd like to question her about it."

"Do you think Josy stole it?"

"I can't think anything else."

"But I'm sure she wouldn't do such a thing."

"That was my opinion, too. But Josy is gone, and so is the money. By the way, who is speaking?"

"It doesn't matter," said Louise, and replaced the receiver. She turned to Jean. "Her story is true to that extent, anyway."

They went back to the study and discussed the affair but decided to withhold judgment for the time being.

"She isn't a thief," declared Jean warmly. "I'm sure of that. It's odd that she wouldn't tell us why the money was sent to her, but it's her own business after all and we have no right to be inquisitive."

The door opened and they looked up to see the homely face of Lettie Briggs in the opening.

"Telephone call for you," said the visitor, trying to appear unconcerned. "You're to call at the Continental House for your Uncle Ned."

"Really?" said Jean, without apparent interest.

"How strange!" murmured Louise.

They did not move from their chairs, but merely smiled at Lettie. They could see Ina Mason hovering in the background.

"I should think you'd be excited," said Lettie. "Your uncle hasn't been in town since Thanksgiving."

"That's so," observed Jean.

"Very true," agreed Louise.

Lettie looked puzzled.

"You're to go down to the Continental House now and ask for him."

Louise smiled.

"Are we?"

"At once?" asked Jean.

"Yes. Right away," declared Lettie, who was beginning to have an uncomfortable suspicion that the practical joke was not working out as she had expected.

"I think I shan't go out tonight," remarked Louise. "It's too cold. And I'm too comfortable here."

"Uncle Ned," said Jean, "can easily wait until tomorrow."

"You're not going down to see him!" exclaimed Lettie Briggs, astounded.

The Dana girls shook their heads solemnly.

"But—but—I thought—do you mean to say you won't go to see your uncle when he comes all the way from Oak Falls?" stammered Lettie.

"Oh, if he did *that*," said Jean, "we'd rush right down to the Continental House. But you see, our Uncle Ned——"

"Is on the Atlantic Ocean just now," said Louise.

"Bringing the *Balaska* back to New York."

The face of Lettie Briggs was a study in chagrin. The maddening indifference of the Dana girls was explained. They had seen through her deceitful joke from the beginning. Deliberately they had sat there and let her make a fool of herself.

"Then there must be a mistake," she muttered.

"You made it," said Jean, "when you thought you could send us on a senseless chase down to the Continental House. After that I suppose we'd have been sent to the State Hotel."

With a wrathful exclamation Lettie Briggs turned, slammed the door, and fled. How the Dana girls had seen through her silly trick she did not know, but of one thing she was certain: they were now enjoying a hearty laugh at her expense, and Lettie Briggs did not like to be laughed at by anyone.

"They knew it was a joke," she stormed, as Ina meekly followed her down the corridor.

"But how could they have known?" inquired Ina in a puzzled voice.

"You must have told someone what we were going to do."

"Why, Lettie, I did not."

"You did. How else could they have known? I suppose they'll tell this all over school." Lettie was furious. "I never felt so humili ated before in all my life. But I'll get back at them. I'll get even yet. I'll make trouble for that homely little witch they pal around with——"

Lettie's voice died away in a startled gasp.

On the wall of the corridor there suddenly loomed a huge, misshapen shadow. Hunchbacked and weird, it hovered mysteriously before them, making a strange and terrifying picture. Lettie stared in fright, and her screams of fear were echoed by Ina as the two girls wheeled about and fled down the hall.

The Dana girls rushed out of their study, alarmed by the screeching and tumultuous disappearance of the pair. They saw Lettie and Ina rushing pell-mell down the stairs at the end of the corridor. At the foot of a flight of steps leading from the upper floor stood Josy Sykes.

The poor cripple gazed at them with stunned, pathetic eyes. She realized that it was her shadow, cast upon the wall by a light at the head of the landing, that had created such panic. Overwhelmed by the knowledge that her deformity had such power to repel and frighten others, she broke into a fit of sobbing.

"They're afraid of me!" she wept. "I knew I shouldn't have come here. Everyone is afraid of me. They don't like me. I'm going to run away again."

The Dana girls did their best to comfort the stricken cripple. They brought her into the study and tried to convince her that she was foolish to allow her affliction to prey upon her mind. It was a long time, however, before Josy Sykes finally dried her eyes and became somewhat cheerful again.

"And you mustn't think of running off," Louise declared. "Don't let a pair of foolish girls like Lettie and Ina frighten you away from Starhurst. It isn't your fault that you are crippled."

"Besides," said Jean, "we want to help you find that money."

"Tomorrow," said Louise.

# CHAPTER IV

## At the Fox Farm

"I'M COLD!" declared Jean Dana, shivering.

"So am I," said Louise, thrusting her hands deep into the pockets of her coat. "And it's going to snow."

"We'll never find that money," said Josy disconsolately. "We can't even find any trace of the fox."

It was mid-afternoon and the white hillside was swept by a bitter north wind. The three girls stood beneath the rocky ledge that had been the scene of the previous afternoon's misadventure and looked at one another in disappointment.

As soon as classes had been dismissed that day, they had hurried out toward the Mohawk Lake trail. For an hour they had searched in vain for the missing thousand-dollar bill and Josy's letter. They had explored the rocks in hopes of finding the den of the black fox, but their search had proven fruitless.

"I don't like to admit that we're beaten," said Louise, "but I'm afraid——"

"We may as well go back to Starhurst," re-

27

marked Josy quietly. "I really didn't have much hope. You have done all you can, but the money is lost, so I'll just have to get along without it the best way possible."

The Dana girls were reluctant to give up the search, but they realized that it was futile. Josy Sykes accepted the loss of her money philosophically. Jean and Louise were surprised to learn that she was more concerned about the missing letter.

"It was very important," she told them as they retraced their steps toward the road, "the most important letter I have ever received in my life."

"But you had read it," said Jean.

"It was very long and there was so much to it that I can't recall all it contained. If I could only remember the address that was written in it, I shouldn't feel so bad. I was just reading the letter for the second time when—when I lost it."

"Our fault, too," declared Louise.

"It wasn't your fault," returned Josy indignantly. "The wind was to blame. And so was the fox. You have done everything anyone could do to help me."

When the girls reached the road, they trudged back in the direction of Penfield. They had not gone very far before they encountered a lanky old gentleman who strode briskly down the highway with the air of one who walks for the pure joy of it.

"Why, it's Mr. Tisdale!" exclaimed Louise.

The gentleman in question beamed with delight when he recognized them.

"The Dana girls!" he cried. "Well, this *is* a surprise."

Mr. Tisdale may have been surprised to see them, but the Dana girls were nothing short of astonished at his appearance. Mr. Tisdale was the father of their English teacher, Miss Amy Tisdale, whose mysterious disappearance had inaugurated the many adventures surrounding *The Secret at Lone Tree Cottage.* When the girls first made his acquaintance, he was a querulous, ill-tempered old man who constantly complained about his health. To find him as he now was, striding along a country road in the face of an incipient snowstorm, seemed beyond their comprehension.

He immediately launched into an enthusiastic account of his latest health fad, and indorsed at great length the virtues of long-distance walking. At the first opportunity Louise managed to change the subject.

"Do you know anything about the habits of foxes, Mr. Tisdale?"

"Foxes? Were we talking about foxes? No, I don't know anything about them. And I don't want to know anything about them, either. Nasty animals. They steal hens, I believe. Why don't you go to the fox farm if you want information about them?"

"Fox farm!" exclaimed Jean. "Where is it?"

"A fellow named Brodsky runs a fox farm about fifteen miles away. Catch the next bus. It will take you right to the front door. Brodsky will tell you all about foxes."

Mr. Tisdale suddenly looked at his watch.

"Bless my soul! I'm behind schedule. Goodbye. Goodbye." And he went away, his coat tails flapping in the breeze.

"He gave us a clue," Louise cried. "Let's go to this fox farm."

"Perhaps that animal escaped from there," said Jean. "I've never heard of any wild foxes near Starhurst. If it were a tame one, perhaps it ran home."

Around the curve in the road there rolled a heavy passenger bus. The Dana girls made their decision without delay.

"We're going," announced Jean, as she signaled to the driver.

Great was their surprise when they climbed on board to find Lettie Briggs and Ina Mason perched in one of the front seats. Lettie sniffed contemptuously when she saw Josy Sykes.

"Some people are hard up for company

when they have to pal around with the hired help,'' she remarked in an audible tone.

Josy flushed, but Jean soon put the snobbish Miss Briggs in her place.

"Just had a wireless from Uncle Ned," she murmured as she passed Lettie's seat. "He sends his love."

Lettie greeted that reminder with haughty silence.

The Dana girls and Josy made their way to the rear seats. They assumed that Lettie and Ina were merely bound for the next town, which was about five miles distant, but it soon became evident that the pair were on a longer journey. Ten miles passed, then twelve, then fifteen, and Lettie and Ina were still on board. Finally the girls saw long lines of high wire fences and whitewashed buildings, and heard the driver call out:

"Brodsky's Fox Farm."

To their unlimited astonishment Lettie Briggs leaned over and pressed the button as a signal to stop.

"Why, they're getting off here, too!" said Josy.

Louise nudged Jean.

"Not a word about the money," she cautioned. "If Lettie and Ina know why we're here, they'll want to take a hand in the search themselves."

"More detective work, I suppose," snapped
Lettie when she saw the others alighting from
the bus. "Not shadowing *me*, I hope."

She was obviously annoyed by the presence
of the Dana girls. The truth of the matter was
that Lettie, who had unlimited pocket money,
was mean and grasping at heart and seldom
neglected an opportunity to save a dollar. She
had set her mind upon having a fox fur piece
and had already driven several Penfield store-
keepers to the point of exasperation by her
haggling over prices. She refused to pay the
lowest compensation asked, and seemed to feel
that because she was Lettie Briggs she should
receive special concessions. Now the economi-
cal young woman was out to teach the store-
keepers a lesson. She would buy her fur
direct from the fox farm.

"You go in, Louise," suggested Jean. "Josy
and I will look around outside while you speak
to the owner."

The elder Dana did as her sister suggested
and followed Lettie and Ina into the office.
The Briggs girl was already talking to Ivan
Brodsky, owner of the farm. He was a fat,
swarthy foreigner of the peasant type. He
bowed politely to Louise.

"Ve haf some nice furs," he was saying to
Lettie. "You come vit me."

He ushered the haughty girl and her chum

into the showroom next to the office, where the furs were laid out upon a table. "You do not mind vaiting?" he inquired of Louise Dana.

"Not at all," the girl assured him.

She listened in amusement as Lettie priced one fur piece after another, invariably declaring that the amount asked was outrageous. Brodsky's prices were quite fair, and it was soon evident that he was not in the least impressed by Lettie and her overbearing manner. She tried to browbeat him when he refused to lower his price on a seventy-five dollar fur, but Brodsky merely shrugged.

"I'll give you sixty dollars and not a cent more," offered Lettie.

"I should give it away first," said Brodsky. "I do you a favor at seventy-five."

"Oh, very well," snapped Lettie. "I'll take it. Here's the money."

She opened her purse and Brodsky went back to the office for change. As he opened the till, he winked solemnly at Louise. A moment later Lettie came out of the showroom with a parcel under her arm.

"I wrapped it up myself," she said. "My change, please."

"Oh, Lady," said Ivan Brodsky, "should I let my customers wrap their own packages? A fur must be wrapped so——"

Then, without handing Lettie her change, he

reached over the counter and took the parcel from under her arm.

"It really doesn't matter," said Lettie.

Ivan Brodsky was already removing the paper, however. When a magnificent black fox fur was revealed, Lettie uttered a cry of feigned astonishment.

"Why, I must have picked up the wrong one by mistake!"

"Hundred dollar mistake," grunted Brodsky.

Without another word he went back into the showroom, put the costly fur back on the table, and returned with the cheaper piece Lettie had purchased. Silently he wrapped it up, handed it to her with her change, and opened the door.

Followed by the frightened Ina, the vanquished Lettie flounced out of the building.

"People got to get up early if they cheat Ivan Brodsky," observed the fur dealer as he closed the door. "Now, young lady, what can I do for you?"

"Have you lost a fox?" demanded Louise.

Brodsky looked startled. He glanced around, as if fearing someone might have overheard.

"Haf you found one?"

"I have seen one," said Louise. "I thought it might have wandered away from this farm."

The dealer sat down heavily.

"I suppose it is mine," he groaned. "Yes, a fox has run away. And what will happen

to me when the farmers find out? If their
chickens are stolen? Not a living soul have I
told about that fox. Bring him back to me,
dead or alive, and I give you five dollars.''

"We thought the animal might have returned,'' said Louise.

Then, without mentioning the thousand-
dollar bill, she explained how the fox had
snatched up an important letter in the meadow
near Mohawk Lake. Ivan Brodsky excitedly
assured her that the fugitive had not returned
to the farm, though in all probability it was
one of his foxes. He begged her to keep his
secret, as he feared the wrath of the farmers
in the vicinity if they knew the animal was at
large.

"I shall leave my address,'' said Louise,
"and if the fox returns, will you please notify
me at once?''

The man promised, and Louise left the
office. She located her sister and the crippled
girl at the back of the farm, looking at some
handsome furry specimens.

"Any news?'' asked Jean.

Louise shook her head, and told of the conversation with Brodsky. Although the girls
were disappointed, they were not discouraged.
Nevertheless, they had little hope that the animal would make its way back with the thousand-dollar bill in its mouth.

They found that they would have to wait half an hour for a bus back to Penfield, so decided to cut across the fields back of the farm and make their way to the railroad station where a train would soon arrive, bound for Penfield. They had walked only a short distance when Josy suddenly cried out:

"Look! What's that thing over there by the fence?"

About two hundred yards away, beyond a clump of trees, the crippled girl had caught sight of a black object against the snow.

"It's our fox!" exclaimed Louise in excitement.

The animal was bounding toward a heap of rocks piled up against the fence. It carried a dead rabbit in its mouth. Swiftly the little beast sped toward a dark opening among the rocks and then vanished.

"Quick!" urged Jean to her sister. "Run back and tell Mr. Brodsky. We've found the fox, all right, and its den, too."

Louise lost no time in hastening back to the fur dealer. In the meantime, Jean and Josy hurried through the snow until they reached the heap of boulders at the fence. Fearing that the animal might escape, they pushed a heavy rock in front of the entrance and sealed the creature in its lair.

"I'll stand on guard," offered Josy, and

leaned over to listen for sounds from the imprisoned animal.

As Jean moved off toward the path to await the coming of the farmhands, she was startled at the really grotesque picture which Josy made. The girl hardly seemed like a human being; rather like a huddled gnome.

The same idea must have sprung into the mind of Brodsky, who had rushed up and caught sight of the deformed figure. Without hesitation the superstitious man slung to his shoulder a rifle which he was carrying and aimed it directly at Josy Sykes!

# CHAPTER V

## A Startling Announcement

Jean screamed. Louise shouted.

Josy turned, stood up, and Ivan Brodsky lowered his rifle.

"A girl!" he gasped, sitting down weakly on the ground. "Oh, Ivan, you are a foolish man. But I cannot help it. When I was a little boy, I was frightened in the woods one day by a strange creature, and ever since——"

Meanwhile, the Dana girls had rushed to Josy's side and were assuring her everything was all right. She did not fully understand that the excited foreigner had really intended to shoot her, and they did not enlighten her.

Presently the humiliated man was once more on his feet, giving directions to his helpers.

"Get dat net ready," he ordered.

The men rolled the rocks aside to expose the frightened animal in its den, and its owner swept the large net over it, just as it leaped forward to escape. The quivering captive was carried back to the farm in triumph. Brodsky was so grateful that he paid more than the promised reward of five dollars.

"You haf saved me much trouble, young ladies," he assured them.

"Give the money to Josy," said Louise.

Meanwhile, Josy Sykes was exploring the rocky lair. She searched in every corner of the animal's refuge, and finally shook her head in disappointment.

"There isn't even a scrap of paper here," she said, her voice trembling. "I never really thought we would be lucky enough to find the bill."

It was a bitter blow, but Josy was courageous. She even tried to smile as the Dana girls sympathized with her.

"It was too much to expect. I'm going to make the best of things even though I've lost my money. I've been poor all my life, so it doesn't make much difference now."

However, they all felt the setback keenly. Having unexpectedly located the fox, it was doubly difficult to bear the disappointment at having lost the money. They were glum and crestfallen when they returned to Starhurst that night.

In their study Jean and Louise discussed the problem of Josy Sykes. The Christmas vacation was only a few days off, and they were already packing for their return to Oak Falls where they were to spend the holidays with Uncle Ned and Aunt Harriet. They knew that there was but little likelihood of Mrs. Crandall's giving the crippled girl a permanent position at Starhurst. Now that Josy had lost all hope of recovering her thousand dollars, the girl had a very uncertain future.

"She won't go back to the Home. And I'm sure Mrs. Crandall won't be able to keep her," said Louise. "I do wish we could do something for her."

Nothing that would further the fortunes of Josy Sykes developed within the next two days, and when Starhurst School finally closed for the Christmas vacation, Jean and Louise bade goodbye to a lonely and pathetic little figure.

"You've been wonderfully good to me," said Josy. "I'll never be able to thank you."

"Please don't try," said Jean. "And we are not going to forget you."

The plight of the Danas' unfortunate little friend was temporarily put out of their minds in the excitement surrounding their return to Oak Falls. Uncle Ned, red-faced and smiling, was at the station to meet them. Aunt Harriet had decorated the big rambling house in their honor, with holly wreaths and cedar branches at every window and a prodigious Christmas tree in the living room. Cora Appel, otherwise known as "Applecore," the clumsy but good-natured servant girl, alternately laughed and cried with delight.

For two days Jean and Louise were engrossed in the joyous flurry of Christmas preparations. The wrapping of presents, the addressing of cards and parcels, the various parties and outings to which they were invited by their friends in Oak Falls sent the hours flying.

"I declare," said Aunt Harriet on Christmas Eve, "I don't know how you keep it up. You'll be all tired out when you go back to school. I'm glad you're staying at home with us this one evening at any rate."

Louise hugged her.

"It wouldn't seem like Christmas Eve unless we spent it with you and Uncle Ned."

Captain Dana lit his pipe and stretched out his legs before the fire.

"We won't be seeing much of you, I'll be bound. You're going to Barnwold Farm tomorrow afternoon, and you'll be staying there, I suppose, for the rest of the week."

Barnwold Farm, near Mount Pleasant, was the home of Miss Bessie Marsh, a cousin of the girls. She was a handsome, practical woman of thirty, who had inherited the property from her parents, and managed it with an efficiency that any man might envy. She was a great favorite with Jean and Louise, and they always looked forward to their visit at her home on Christmas Day.

The Dana household rang with laughter next morning. Uncle Ned, officiating as Santa Claus, distributed the gifts piled at the foot of the shimmering tree. The room was littered with gaily colored wrapping paper. Jean and Louise had been well remembered by their aunt and uncle, while in their turn they had come from Starhurst with numerous pretty gifts for each member of the household.

Jean and Louise had each sent a little gift to Josy Sykes at Starhurst, and were touched and surprised to find that the crippled girl had not forgotten them. Josy had evidently spent a part of the reward she had received from Ivan Brodsky, for there were two neatly wrapped packages for the Dana girls, which had arrived in the mail the day before. There was also a letter which read:

"MY DEAR, DEAR FRIENDS: "I hope you are having a happy Christmas. This little note is to send my best wishes and to say goodbye. I shall not be here when you return to school. Mrs. Crandall has been very kind, but she does not need me any more, and I am to leave at the end of the week. With many thanks for all the kindness you have shown me, I am,

Gratefully,

JOSY SYKES."

"But she can't go away like that!" exclaimed Louise. "Where will she go? How can we ever find her again?"

"I have it!" said Jean impulsively. "Perhaps Cousin Bessie will let us invite her to Barnwold Farm."

When they talked to their relative over the phone a few minutes later, they found her to be instantly sympathetic.

"The poor child!" she exclaimed. "Spending Christmas in a lonely school! By all means bring her with you. I'm expecting you by dinner time tonight, of course."

"We'll be there," Louise assured her. "And Josy will be with us."

Happy at the prospect that they would be able to lend some brightness to Josy's Christmas, the Dana girls dispatched a telegram to their friend at Starhurst, telling her of the invitation and asking her to meet them at Mount Pleasant station that afternoon. As they did so, they had no idea that their well-meant effort to brighten the unfortunate girl's Christmas was to have such strange and far-reaching consequences as later events proved.

When they alighted from the train at four o'clock, Josy Sykes was waiting for them on the platform. Tears of gladness sprang to the eyes of the crippled girl as Jean and Louise greeted her.

"It really seems like Christmas now."

When they arrived at Barnwold Farm, they were warmly greeted by Bessie Marsh, whose tact and good humor quickly put Josy at her ease.

"I'm so glad the girls told me about you," said Cousin Bessie.

Josy's natural shyness soon wore off. Curled up on a big sofa before the fireplace in the living room of the farmhouse, it was not long before the crippled girl began to beam with happiness.

Cousin Bessie, jolly and friendly, told anecdotes and teased the Dana girls about several little incidents which she recalled. The crippled girl joined in the laughter and merriment.

"A friend of mine," said Cousin Bessie suddenly, "had an unusual experience the other day. He went hunting—and what do you think he brought home?"

"A bear," said Jean.

"A cold in the head," laughed Louise.

"A frostbitten ear," suggested Josy.

"You'd never guess," declared Miss Marsh. "He went out hunting rabbits near Lake Mohawk, and brought home a thousand-dollar bill!"

# CHAPTER VI

## HARSH WORDS

COUSIN BESSIE was astonished at the effect of her words. She had created a sensation. The Dana girls gasped. As for Josy, she turned white and sprang up from the couch where she was seated.

"A thousand dollars!" she cried. "Oh, it's mine. It's mine."

Then, with a low moan she fell to the floor in a faint.

Jean and Louise hastily knelt beside the insensible girl to render first aid. Cousin Bessie, puzzled and alarmed, ran from the room, but returned in a moment followed by her housekeeper, Mrs. Graves, carrying some cold water and smelling salts. The girls had lifted Josy back onto the divan and were rubbing her hands and wrists in an effort to revive her.

"What *is* the matter?" asked Cousin Bessie. "I can't understand it. What did she mean by saying 'It's mine'? Just because Bart Wheeler found a thousand dollars——"

"But it's Josy's money," cried Louise. "It must be. She lost a thousand-dollar bill and a

45

letter in a field near Lake Mohawk a few days ago. No wonder she fainted."

Bessie Marsh was immediately excited.

"I never heard of such a thing!" she declared. "Yes, this money was in one bill, and there was a strange letter with it, too. Mr. Wheeler is Constance Melbourne's secretary. You've heard of her—the famous artist."

Both girls nodded in the affirmative.

"It seems almost too good to be true," said Jean. "I hope he hasn't spent the money," added Louise. "Josy had given up all hope of ever seeing it again."

The housekeeper was busily and tenderly trying to bring the cripple back to consciousness. Her efforts were rewarded when the girl's eyelids flickered and she moaned softly.

"She'll be all right before long," said Mrs. Graves.

"I'm going to telephone Bart Wheeler this very minute," announced Bessie Marsh. "I'll ask him to bring that money over here. It's the oddest coincidence——"

Marvelling, she hurried from the room. Jean and Louise turned their attention to Josy, who opened her eyes and looked up at them appealingly.

"What has happened to me?" she asked in a weak voice. "I must have fainted."

Suddenly she struggled in an effort to sit up.

"Oh, I remember now. My money. Someone found my thousand-dollar bill."

"Cousin Bessie is telephoning to the man now," said Louise in a soothing voice.

"She is going to ask him to come over and talk to you," added Jean.

"Of course, it might not be your money after all," Louise remarked cautiously.

It would be tragic, she felt, if Josy built her hopes high, only to suffer another disappointment.

"We'll just have to wait until Mr. Wheeler tells us all about it."

Mrs. Graves piled cushions under Josy's head and drew a coverlet over her.

"Don't excite yourself, my dear," she advised kindly. "Just try to rest quietly."

Josy closed her eyes and sighed.

"I hope there isn't any mistake," she murmured.

In less than half an hour a smart little roadster slid to a stop in the driveway of Barnwold Farm, and a handsome man in an ulster and rakish-looking hat stepped out and came hurriedly up the walk. The person in question was Bart Wheeler, a man in his early thirties, artistic and sensitive.

Cousin Bessie had already explained to the girls that he acted as secretary and business manager to Constance Fleurette Melbourne,

the world-famous portrait painter and artist.
Miss Melbourne, when she was not travelling,
lived in a quaint, cobblestone towered studio
home near Barnwold Farm.

Miss Marsh met him at the door.

"Hello, Bessie. What's all the excitement?"

"Bart, we've found the owner of the
thousand-dollar bill you picked up," she replied.

"Well, that's good," rejoined Mr. Wheeler.
"I'm sure I shouldn't care to lose a thousand
dollars if I had it. Where's the lucky person?"

Cousin Bessie escorted him into the living
room. He bowed politely when she introduced
him to the Dana girls, but looked puzzled when
Miss Marsh indicated Josy on the sofa.

"And this is Miss Sykes, the girl who lost
the thousand dollars," he said, musingly.

"Did you really find my money?" asked
Josy eagerly. "Did you bring it with you?"

"Yes," said Bart Wheeler slowly, looking
steadfastly at the figure on the sofa. "I found
a thousand-dollar bill and a letter."

He was silent for a moment, and the Danas
wondered what he was thinking about. Presently he spoke.

"But I think there must be a mistake somewhere."

"A mistake?" gasped Josy.

"I'm afraid the letter and bill belong to someone else," said Bart Wheeler, weighing each word.

"Oh, that isn't so!" declared Louise indignantly. "Jean and I were with her when she lost it."

"Perhaps so," said Bart Wheeler. "But I still think there is a mistake."

"How could there be?" came from Jean.

"How did you know she was the rightful owner in the first place?" the man asked.

The Dana girls were stunned by this accusation. There was no misunderstanding Bart Wheeler's meaning. He was insinuating that Josy was either impersonating the owner of the money, or that she had come by it unlawfully in the beginning.

"Bart!" exclaimed Miss Marsh sharply. "You have no right to say such a thing."

"I have every right in the world," said the secretary. "I have proof."

Louise and Jean looked at the girl on the sofa. She had drawn the coverlet up around her and was staring wild-eyed at the speaker, fear and anguish on her drawn face.

"The money doesn't belong to her," continued Wheeler, pointing toward Josy. "I'm sure of it. There was a letter with the bill. The money belonged to Miss Josephine Sykes, all right, *but I think this is not Miss Sykes!*"

# CHAPTER VII

## STRANGE HAPPENINGS

JEAN and Louise were speechless at Bart Wheeler's announcement. Had they been befriending an impostor?

Bessie Marsh was the first to speak.

"What did the letter say?" she demanded.

"It stated," answered the secretary, "that the owner of the money was a deformed and hopeless cripple. This girl is no cripple."

With a sob of humiliation, Josy flung aside the coverlet and rose from the couch. When she stood up, revealing her deformed figure, Bart Wheeler uttered a startled gasp. An expression of amazement and horror crossed his face.

Josy could stand no more. Interpreting it as an expression of revulsion at her misshapen and ugly form, she burst into tears and hurried out of the room.

"Bart Wheeler!" stormed Bessie Marsh. "Of all the tactless, blundering people on the face of the earth——"

"But I tell you I didn't know—I didn't mean —oh, what have I done?" stammered Wheeler.

The room was in confusion. Louise and Jean ran after Josy to comfort her. They realized that Bart Wheeler's expression was caused by his embarrassment when he learned that he had wrongly accused the girl of trying to claim the lost money.

The strain, however, had been too much for Josy. They found her weeping bitterly in the hall.

"I'm just a hopeless, unwanted girl, and cause trouble wherever I go," she declared disconsolately.

Josy's notion that she had caused trouble was unfortunately borne out by the fact that the incident had evidently precipitated a bitter quarrel between Cousin Bessie and Bart Wheeler. Always an outspoken woman, Miss Marsh could be heard warmly berating her friend for his tactless mistake. He in turn resentfully defended himself, and before long the argument was at its height. It ended when Bart Wheeler snapped:

"There's the money and the letter. Give it to the girl."

"I should think you would give it to her yourself and apologize at the same time!"

"Goodbye. I'm not coming back."

"Don't."

Bart Wheeler, flushed and angry, strode out into the hall.

"I'm sorry, Miss Sykes," he said curtly. Then he flung open the door and vanished.

Josy was trembling with embarrassment. She felt that she was directly responsible for this heated quarrel between Miss Marsh and her friend. Even when Cousin Bessie guided her back into the living room and gave her the letter and the thousand-dollar bill, she could muster up very little enthusiasm.

"Aren't you glad?" asked Jean. "I think I'd be turning handsprings if I were to lose a thousand dollars and someone returned it to me like this."

Josy's face was sad.

"I'm glad to get the money, of course. But this letter——"

"Bad news?" asked Cousin Bessie.

"Disappointing news," confessed Josy. "It's from the only relative I have in the world."

Josy Sykes was a moody, reticent girl. On several occasions she had seemed on the point of telling Jean and Louise more about her past life but had always hesitated when on the point of doing so. Beyond a sketchy account of her life at the Home, the Dana girls really knew very little about their friend. She told them now that the letter was from her uncle, Joseph Sykes. Further than that she volunteered little information.

"I wonder if I'll ever see him again," said Josy.

Then, fearing that she had been talking too much, she checked herself just when about to confide in her friends the reason for her mysterious uncle sending her the thousand-dollar bill.

In a short time other guests arrived, and soon the unpleasant incident of the money was forgotten.

The dinner party was a great success. Josy, evidently resolved that her hostess should not regret having invited her, had fought down her mood of despondency and was among the gayest at the table. After dinner, at Jean's urging, she helped entertain the guests by whistling and singing.

The Dana girls were astonished at Josy's talent. She had a good voice and her whistling was as finished as that of any stage performer. Nevertheless, she seemed to take neither pride nor pleasure in her accomplishment.

"It isn't useful," she said dolefully.

Josy went to bed early, and Jean and Louise accepted Cousin Bessie's invitation to talk over the events of the afternoon. Jean and Louise had told their cousin the odd circumstances of their meeting with Josy.

"I _do_ wish we could do something for her," said Cousin Bessie. "Financially, she has no

immediate worries—thanks to Bart Wheeler—
but she should have some sort of work that will
help her take her mind off her troubles."

"Josy believes she is a failure," observed
Louise. "She thinks nothing can ever compen-
sate for her being a cripple."

"If some way could be found for her to make
use of her talent," said Cousin Bessie, "I
think she would be much happier. As long as
she feels that she is a burden to people, she
will always be despondent."

"She felt bad because you quarreled with
Mr. Wheeler," ventured Jean.

"It was Bart's fault. He made her feel terrible. He might have known that I shouldn't
have asked him to bring the money and the
letter here unless I was quite sure Josy was
the rightful owner. I suppose I shouldn't have
lost my temper. Poor Bart. He threatened to
go away forever."

"He is a very handsome man," said Louise.

"And an artist to his finger tips," declared
Bessie. "I think the world of Bart, really.
Miss Melbourne says she couldn't get along
without him. She isn't very practical, and he
manages all her business affairs. I'm sorry
she wasn't here tonight, but she telephoned
to say she was just recovering from a cold."

At this moment the doorbell rang sharply
and loudly. It was not the easy, casual ring

of some chance caller, but an imperative, agitated trilling that sent Mrs. Graves bustling to answer it. Immediately a tall, commanding figure swept into the room.

"Why, Constance!" exclaimed Miss Marsh in surprise. "What brings you here?"

Constance Fleurette Melbourne's appearance was in accord with her world-renowned reputation as being one of the greatest of American artists. She was very tall and slender, a woman of forty-five, with hair prematurely white. Just now she was excited and distressed.

"My dear!" she cried. "I've just had the most upsetting and nerve-wracking experience. What in the world has gone wrong with Bart Wheeler?"

"Bart?" exclaimed Bessie. "Why—well, we had a little quarrel——"

"A *little* quarrel?" said Miss Melbourne. "Why, the man has left me. The only capable secretary I ever had. I was listening to a mystery play on the radio tonight—the weirdest thing, all shouts and groans and screams and revolver shots—when he rushed into the studio tower. The man looked as if he had been wading in snowdrifts. His face was white as a sheet. His clothes were wet. He was ghastly. And he simply said, 'I'm going away and I'm not coming back.' Then he ran upstairs to his room and packed his things."

Miss Marsh rose to her feet. Her face was pitiful to behold.

"He packed?"

"He crammed some clothes into a suitcase. I couldn't get a word out of him. Then he snatched up the valise and ran down the tower stairs. He stumbled and fell on the steps, picked himself up, called out, 'I'm not coming back,' and away he went. Has the man gone crazy?"

"He told me he was going away!" cried Bessie despairingly. "I didn't think he meant it though."

"But that isn't all," continued Miss Melbourne. "Mammy Cleo, my cook, came running out of the kitchen a few minutes later, and when I told her that Bart had left, she became nearly hysterical and said an evil spirit had stolen him. Imagine that! She said she had seen a strange, supernatural figure in the snow in the shadow of the tower about fifteen minutes earlier. I declare I don't know what to make of it."

"A strange, supernatural figure!" said Louise in awe. She looked quickly at Jean.

"Mammy Cleo said it must have been an evil spirit, because it didn't look like either man or woman. It was twisted and deformed——"

"Josy!" cried Jean.

She ran from the room, with Louise close at her heels. The two girls rushed up the stairs and rapped sharply at Josy's room. There was no response. Jean thrust the door open and switched on the light.

The place was empty!

"Just as I thought," Louise declared. "She has run away."

"We'll have to follow her," gasped Jean.

In their haste and excitement the girls had no time to consider the strange features of the affair—Bart Wheeler's disappearance, the story of the deformed figure in the shadow of the tower, and now the flight of Josy Sykes! What connection, if any, lay between these events they could not imagine.

As they hurried back downstairs, the door-bell rang frantically. Mrs. Graves was bustling into the hall as the Dana girls reached the foot of the stairway. When the housekeeper opened the door, the light fell on the rolling eyes and frightened face of an elderly negro.

"I'se got a hawss heah, Ma'am," he stammered. "It belongs t' Miss Mah'sh."

Cousin Bessie, overhearing the man's words, hurried from the living room.

"My mare?" she cried. "Where did you get it?"

The man rolled his eyes again. He stuttered

and stammered so much that his words were scarcely intelligible. It was evident that he was badly frightened. Out of his terrified mumblings, however, they managed to learn that while he had been standing at the crossroads near Mount Pleasant, a weird, deformed figure had ridden up to him on horseback.

A hunchback had descended from the saddle and asked him to return the mare to Miss Marsh. A moment later the cripple had boarded a bus that had been approaching, and the negro had been left with the animal.

"Ma'am," he said earnestly, "if it hadn't been fo' dat hawss, Ah would have thought Ah dreamed it."

Cousin Bessie turned a startled face toward the Dana girls.

"A hunchback!" she exclaimed. "Why, it must have been Josy."

Louise nodded gravely.

"It *was* Josy. She isn't in her room."

"But why—why should she run away?" Cousin Bessie was utterly bewildered. "She must have taken my mare from the stable so she could ride out to the bus line. And if what Mammy Cleo says is true, she must have been at the Studio Tower."

"It's too involved for me," confessed Jean. "I think Louise and I had better bring the mare around to the stable. Then we'll sit

down and talk things over. Perhaps Josy will
come back.''

In their hearts the Dana girls felt that the
cripple would not return.

The colored man hurried off, still mumbling
to himself about his encounter with the hunchback. It was obvious that his superstitious
mind clung to the belief that there was an element of black magic about the whole business,
and that the strange, dwarfed figure had not
been entirely human after all.

Jean and Louise brought the mare around to
the stable. When they came back to the house
a few minutes later, Cousin Bessie was telling
Miss Melbourne the story of the hunchback.

''There is a mystery about the girl,'' con-
tended Bessie. ''The money and the letter
that Bart Wheeler found belonged to her. But
who would send a friendless orphan a thousand-
dollar bill? And why? She claims that the
money was dispatched by her only surviving
relative, yet if he is wealthy enough to send
her all that money, it seems odd that he should
have left her in a Home.''

The Dana girls were surprised at the expression on Miss Melbourne's face. She was very
white. She looked ill. One slender hand was
gripping the back of a chair tensely.

''Did she—did she ever tell you the name of
this relative?'' asked Miss Melbourne.

"His name was almost the same as her own," said Louise. "Joseph Sykes."

Miss Melbourne closed her eyes.

"Joseph Sykes!" she murmured. Suddenly she swayed, and the girls thought she was about to faint, but she recovered with an effort and staggered toward the hall. "It is more than I can stand," they heard her mutter. "Bessie—I'm going home."

She stumbled to the door.

"But you can't go alone, Constance," cried Miss Marsh. "What is the matter?"

"We'll go with her," offered Louise. "I'm afraid she isn't well."

The Dana girls accompanied the artist through the snow to her quaint, picturesque towered home. It was not any great distance, but the artist seemed to find it extremely difficult to get there. She walked slowly and wearily, like one whose strength is utterly spent.

Although the girls were burning with curiosity as to why the story of Josy Sykes should have had such a peculiar effect upon the famous artist, Miss Melbourne explained nothing. She scarcely uttered a word on that strange, halting journey through the darkness and snow. Not until she reached her home with its studio tower looming black against the sky did she seem to be aware of their presence.

"It was good of you to come with me," said Miss Melbourne mechanically. "I shouldn't have gone out in the snow like this."

She pressed her hand to her forehead. There was a wild, shining look in her eyes.

"Oh, find that child! Find that child!" she sobbed.

She swayed, tried to maintain her equilibrium, and then, in the shadow of the tower, fell unconscious.

# CHAPTER VIII

## The Mystery Deepens

As Jean and Louise Dana carried the unconscious woman into her home, they realized that they had stumbled upon one of the strangest mysteries in their experience.

"Find that child!"

They recalled the strange conduct of Miss Melbourne when she had heard the story of Josy Sykes. Now this heartbroken command puzzled them. It could have reference only to Josy. How the talented and wealthy artist could possibly be connected with the pathetic cripple they could not guess, yet it was obvious that some hidden thread existed among the lives of Josy, Miss Melbourne, and the missing Bart Wheeler.

Mammy Cleo, a huge colored woman, met them as they carried her mistress into the Tower.

"I'se gwine call de doctah," she announced after one glance at the lady. "She's sick, she is. Shouldn't nebbah have gone outside dis doah tonight," she went on, as she helped them carry Miss Melbourne upstairs to bed.

The lower part of the building consisted of one huge room, towered to the roof, which was used as the studio and living room, while the bedrooms were upstairs in the rear.

Miss Melbourne did not entirely recover consciousness. She stirred restlessly on the bed, moaning as she had done before her collapse:

"Find that child! Oh, you *must* find her——"

Although the house was warm, it failed to keep the artist from shivering. The girls realized that she was far from well. When Mammy Cleo bustled back into the bedroom after having telephoned to Mount Pleasant for the doctor, Jean and Louise gave what help they could. Miss Melbourne was undressed and put to bed. Mammy Cleo's round, shiny face was grave.

"Black cat crossed mah path today," she said portentously. "Allus means bad luck. Whaffor she keep talkin' 'bout a chile? 'Fin' dat chile,' she says. No chillen 'roun' dis place."

Although the Dana girls did not share Mammy Cleo's superstition about the black cat, the doctor's arrival brought them to a realization that bad luck had indeed befallen the Studio Tower. Miss Melbourne's condition showed no improvement; in fact, she grew rapidly worse. She seemed to be in a sort of delirium, repeating Josy's name over and over again, and time and again declaring that the crippled girl must be located at all cost.

The doctor, an elderly, soft-spoken man from Mount Pleasant, seated himself by the bedside.

"She was just recovering from a bad cold," explained Louise, "and went out tonight. She wasn't very warmly dressed."

The doctor shook his head.

"Miss Melbourne is very ill," he announced. "She has pneumonia."

They were shocked into silence.

"She can't be moved to the hospital now," continued the doctor, "but if her life is to be saved, she must have the best of care. She will need a nurse with her, day and night."

"If there is anything we can do," volunteered Jean, "we'll be glad to help."

"Very little, I'm afraid. It was almost suicidal for her to go out in the snow on a night like this. She took a very bad chill and seems to have suffered a shock of some kind as well. I'll call up Miss Robertson and ask her to come out right away. She is a very capable nurse."

He left the room quickly, and a few moments later they heard him at the telephone. Mammy Cleo's eyes were round with fear and she wrung her fat hands helplessly.

"I think we'd better go," whispered Jean.

Louise nodded. They had done what they

could, and they knew that if they were to remain, their presence might only add to the confusion of the household. Sadly they returned to Barnwold Farm. So much had happened since their arrival at Cousin Bessie's home that they felt bewildered in the face of the mystery that seemed to deepen with every passing moment.

"I never went through such an evening in my life!" declared Louise. "First of all, Josy recovers her money. Then she runs away. Mr. Wheeler quarrels with Bessie and then *he* runs away."

"And now Miss Melbourne comes down with pneumonia, and she can't tell us what she knows about Josy. But she knows something —that's plain enough."

"What could it be? Josy didn't give any inkling that she had ever heard of Miss Melbourne before."

As they approached the house, they saw a light in Miss Marsh's window. Against the drawn shade they could see the figure of their cousin silhouetted, pacing to and fro. When they hurried to her room to tell her about Miss Melbourne's collapse and serious illness, they found that Bessie had been crying. In her hand she clutched a photograph.

"Pneumonia!" she cried. "Oh, this is terrible!" She sank into a chair. "Troubles

never come singly. As if it wasn't enough to
have lost Bart——''

The photograph slipped from her hand.
She began to cry softly. Jean knelt and re-
covered the picture, which was one of Bart
Wheeler.

In a flash the girls realized why their cousin
had been so distressed and upset by her quarrel that afternoon. Louise slipped an arm
around Bessie's shoulders.

''Do you care for him so very much?'' she
whispered.

''I—I'm engaged to him,'' sobbed Bessie.
''We've been engaged for three weeks. And
—and now—I've sent him away—oh, what a
fool I was to quarrel with him——''

The girls were stunned by this revelation.
The flight of Bart Wheeler now assumed a
new significance. What mystery lay behind his
hasty departure they did not know, but they
felt that there was something more than a
mere lovers' quarrel back of it all. Their
hearts went out to their cousin in her distress,
for Bessie blamed herself for the breach with
her fiancé and upbraided herself constantly for
her quick temper. She was taking Bart's
threat seriously, and firmly believed that he
would never return.

Overwrought by excitement, Bessie had given
way completely. She wept until she was ex-

hausted. Jean and Louise comforted her as
well as they could.

"I am sure he went away for some other
reason than because he quarreled with you,"
said Louise.

"I believe so too," declared Jean. "If he
did, you're well rid of him. It's too foolish.
There was something else. He'll be back
again."

"B-but he said he wouldn't—ever," sobbed
Bessie.

She became a little less sad, however, when
the girls insisted that Bart Wheeler's departure had something to do with the disappearance of Josy Sykes. She was completely
mystified when they told her of Miss Melbourne's distraught pleas to "find that child,"
but could throw no light on that part of the
puzzle.

"I can't understand why she should be interested in Josy's case. As far as I know, she
had never heard of the girl," said Bessie.
"She did act oddly when I told her Josy's
story, though. Perhaps it was because she was
so ill."

Bessie was in a more composed frame of
mind when the Dana girls finally bade her
good night and went on down the hall toward
the guest room.

"One thing is certain," declared Jean.

"We've stumbled on a mystery that has my head in a whirl. This affair is a good deal more complicated than anything we've ever tackled before."

"She seemed very upset when she heard about Josy. We must follow up every possible clue, Jean, if we are going to get Josy back for Miss Melbourne——"

"And Bart Wheeler for Bessie."

"I do wish Josy had told us more about that letter. If we could find this man Joseph Sykes, he might be able to throw more light on the affair," said Louise. "And if we could only find Bart Wheeler, he would be able to help us. He read Josy's letter after he found it."

As they approached their door, Jean suddenly spied a folded slip of paper.

"Why, what's this?" she exclaimed, as she knelt and picked it up. "It was halfway beneath our door."

"It's a note!"

Jean unfolded it quickly. Her eyes swept over the few words written on the sheet, and then she turned to her sister in bewilderment.

"It's from Josy Sykes," said Jean. "But what a strange, strange note it is!"

# CHAPTER IX

## THE VEILED PORTRAIT

JOSY's farewell note was, indeed, a strange message. It consisted of only a few lines:

"MY DEAR FRIENDS: Please do not think unkindly of me, but I feel that I should go away. All the world hates me. I'm unwanted and I cause trouble wherever I go. Mr. Wheeler knows my secret sorrow. He can tell you, and then you will understand why I could not stay here any longer. I am everlastingly grateful to you for your kindness to me."

"Mr. Wheeler knew!" gasped Louise. "There must have been some secret in that letter he found."

"But why should it have prompted him to disappear as well?"

Their cousin's door opened. Bessie looked out at them.

"What's the matter?" she asked.

"We found a note from Josy."

Bessie hastened down the hall. When she

read the plaintive message, she was even more
puzzled and disturbed than the Dana girls.
The note seemed to prove beyond all doubt that
Bart Wheeler's flight had been prompted by
something more than his quarrel with Bessie.
There was little consolation in this, however.

"I can't understand it," declared Bessie.
"Bart must have read the letter immediately
after he found it on his hunting trip, but it
didn't seem to disturb him then. I do wish
we could find Josy. She would be able to throw
some light on it."

They were at a loss to know where Josy
might have gone. The Dana girls knew that
she had no friends and relatives other than the
uncle she had mentioned and the officials of the
Home for Crippled Children.

"She might have gone to her uncle," Jean
suggested.

"She might have returned to the Home,"
said Louise. "Perhaps she wanted to clear
herself of the robbery."

But these were mere guesses. They realized
that Josy, with one thousand dollars in her
possession, had no need of going to any place
where she was known. The money would sus-
tain her for a long time.

Bessie had a faint but stubborn hope that
Bart Wheeler might repent of his decision and
return to the Studio Tower. Next morning,

when they telephoned for news of Miss Melbourne, they were told that Wheeler's disappearance was as great a mystery as ever.

News from Miss Melbourne's bedside was not at all encouraging. She was critically ill, still delirious, and in the care of day and night nurses. Her life literally hung by a thread.

Word of some of the strange events of the previous evening had spread beyond the confines of Barnwold Farm, according to Mrs. Graves, the housekeeper. The grocery boy had informed her that the colored folks in the vicinity had told and retold fragments of the stories of the dwarf, the black mare at the crossroads, and the rantings of Miss Melbourne until they had built up a monstrous and weird legend about the affair. Their superstitious minds had magnified and distorted the various incidents, whispering that a dark and gruesome mystery shrouded the "goings-on" at the Studio Tower and at Barnwold Farm.

The Dana girls had heard rumors of this distorted gossip that afternoon when they decided to walk over to the Tower and inquire about Miss Melbourne. On the way they encountered two colored youngsters who gazed at them in pop-eyed terror and scuttled to the side of the road.

"What's the matter?" asked Jean with a smile. "You surely aren't afraid of us?"

"Yass'm. Yass'm. We's scairt of you folks," piped one of the children.

"Why?" demanded Louise.

"My mammy she say dey wuz a dwa'f at Missy Bessie's place. A dwa'f widout no head."

"Ridin' on a hawss!" supplemented the other.

"A headless dwarf riding on horseback!" cried Jean. "Do you believe that?"

"Yass'm, we done b'lieves it. Missy Melbourne, she see dat dwa'f and she done went crazy, dat's what my mammy says, and Mistah Wheeler he done jump clean off de top ob de towah an' he ain't been seen since."

"It's a better story than the original at any rate," laughed Louise as they went on their way, with the youngsters peeping at them in awe from behind a fence post. "They certainly managed to get the facts twisted."

When they reached the Tower, they were received by Mammy Cleo, who welcomed them with delight. This faithful old servant had been having her own troubles, what with "mah kitchen jes' ovahrun wid nu'ses, who keeps givin' o'dahs till Ah don' know wheah Ah'm at." The old cook was very talkative and evidently glad to see them, for her position of authority in the household had been seriously threatened by the arrival of the nurses, and she was eager to air her grievances. She blamed everything on the black cat.

"Minute Ah seed dat black cat," she declared, "Ah knowed trouble was brewin'. An' den trouble begins bustin' right in mah face."

Miss Melbourne, she told them sadly, had suffered a bad night. The doctor and Miss Robertson, the nurse, had remained constantly at her bedside, making no secret of the fact that her condition was critical. It was considered a blessing that the Dana girls had accompanied the patient home from Barnwold. Otherwise, Miss Melbourne might have wandered about in the snow and suffered exposure that would have caused her death.

"She's not gwine die!" declared Mammy Cleo firmly. "She's gwine get better. Pow'-ful sma'ht lady, she is."

The devoted servant, who had been in the artist's service for many years, escorted the girls around the strange, towered studio. They were entranced by the many pictures they saw on the walls, representing Constance Melbourne's finest work. As the old servant guided them about the great room she told them little stories about the different paintings on view.

In a distant nook of the studio Jean caught sight of a heavy purple drapery. Beneath the covering she could see the legs of an easel.

"Is that the picture on which Miss Melbourne has just been working?"

Mammy Cleo shook her head.

"Ah calls dat her *sad* picture," said the colored woman. "It's allus kep' covered up."

"But why is that?" inquired Louise, interested.

"Dunno," replied Mammy Cleo. "Whenebber Miss Melbourne feels sad, she does a li'l bit ob work on dat picture. She's kep' it in dis corner for a long, long time."

"May we see it?"

Cautiously Mammy Cleo raised the velvet drapery. The girls gazed in awe and admiration at the picture that was revealed to them.

It proved to be a magnificent portrait of a handsome young man. The beauty of the workmanship seemed to leap at them from the canvas. Although they had just seen many fine portraits in the studio they knew instantly that this was the masterpiece.

"Why, it's *wonderful!*" cried Jean. "It's one of the most beautiful portraits I've ever seen."

"Why does she keep it covered up?" asked Louise.

Mammy Cleo shook her head and replaced the drapery.

"Ah don' ask no questions 'bout dat picture," she said.

Jean wrinkled her brow. Here was another mystery. She had just observed a strange thing about the "sad picture." It was the only portrait in the studio without Constance Melbourne's signature.

# CHAPTER X

## A THIEF

THEIR speculations regarding the mysterious portrait were interrupted at this moment by the entrance of a brisk, dark-haired woman in the uniform of a nurse. Mammy Cleo, after hastily restoring the drapery covering the picture, introduced the newcomer to the Dana girls as Miss Robertson.

Miss Robertson, the night nurse, was a friendly, agreeable woman and chatted readily with the girls. She said that Miss Melbourne was "a very sick person," but that she had a good constitution which might enable her to pass the crisis successfully.

"Are you comfortable here?" asked Louise. "It must be very lonesome at night."

"Yes, it's lonesome enough," agreed the nurse. "Night duty always is, in a case like this. However, it's my job, so I can't complain. I wish I had never left my old hospital position, though."

"What hospital was that?" Jean asked.

"I was head nurse in the Home and Hospital for Crippled Children, at Bonny Lake."

Miss Robertson was surprised at the effect of this simple statement. The Dana girls gasped with amazement.

"Then you must have known Josy Sykes," exclaimed Jean.

Miss Robertson looked grave.

"Poor Josy," she said. "Yes, I knew her very well indeed. Is she a friend of yours?"

"She was staying with us at Barnwold Farm," said Louise. A warning look from Jean, however, checked her from making any further revelations about Josy. "Why did she leave the Home? Is it true that she was accused of stealing some money?"

"That was an unfortunate affair," declared the nurse. "Personally, I don't believe Josy had anything to do with the loss of the money. Just because she was working in the office when the receipts from the benefit were being counted doesn't prove that she was the guilty party. It was foolish of her to run away."

"But they didn't find any trace of the thief."

"Josy Sykes was innocent, I'm sure of that," Miss Robertson declared firmly. "I have my own ideas about that incident. It's my opinion that Mrs. Rita Rye knows more about it than she pretends to."

"Who is she?" asked Louise. "Does she work at the Home?"

"Not she. Mrs. Rye is one of the trustees,

and about the most snobbish, disagreeable woman I ever met in my life." It was plain from the nurse's tone that she had scant affection for this particular individual. "She used to be a vaudeville actress before she married old Mr. Rye. She wanted him only for his money, of course, because he was old enough to be her grandfather and had one foot in the grave when she met him. He died last year. With all her airs I think she's less wealthy than she pretends to be."

"I'm glad you believe Josy is innocent," said Jean.

"Josy isn't a thief, poor child," declared Miss Robertson. "It was Mrs. Rye who first suggested that she might have been the guilty party. There was a reason for that, I'm sure."

Nurse Robertson's unshattered faith in Josy's innocence made the Dana girls more determined than ever to locate their missing friend. It was their opinion now that the girl's sensitive spirit had caused her to exaggerate the nature of the suspicions against her.

"If she had remained to fight it out," said the nurse firmly, "I'm sure she would have convinced them that she didn't steal the money."

Miss Robertson glanced at her wrist watch.

"I must take my patient's temperature," she said briskly, and hurried away. "Come around and talk to me again," she flung back over her shoulder.

The Dana girls did not want to disturb Mammy Cleo, so they found their way out alone. They were greatly cheered by Miss Robertson's belief in Josy's blamelessness.

"It might have made all the difference in the world if we could have talked to the poor girl before she went away," said Louise. "I think she had the idea that everyone at the Home suspected her."

As they were leaving the Tower, they saw an odd-looking figure coming down the path. It proved to be a fat, flabby-faced young man wearing a broad-brimmed black hat, an Inverness cape and a Windsor tie. A cane hung over his wrist, and he advanced in a slouchy, indolent manner, with the air of one to whom time is no object. When he confronted the girls, he removed his hat with a languid flourish.

"How do you do?" he said, in a weary voice. "This is the home of Miss Constance Melbourne, is it not?"

"Yes," replied Jean. "But Miss Melbourne can't see anyone. She is very ill."

The young man shrugged.

"I'm not calling on Miss Melbourne. Do you know if Mr. Wheeler is at home?"

"Mr. Wheeler is away."

The young man stirred up the snow with his cane.

"Dear, dear!" he exclaimed petulantly. "How annoying! I really must see him at once."

"I'm afraid you can't," said Louise. "We don't know where he is."

"Don't tell me I've made this journey for nothing!" exclaimed the stranger, evidently chagrined. "Who may you be? Are you related to Miss Melbourne?"

"No. We are from Barnwold Farm," replied Jean. "We are cousins of Miss Marsh."

The young man brightened up. "Ah, yes," he said. "Dear Bessie Marsh. Well, if you are going to the farm now, I'll offer you a ride."

His car, a cheap and venerable roadster, was parked nearby. The girls protested that it was only a short walk, but the young man insisted upon driving them.

"As a matter of fact," he said, "I should like to see Miss Marsh anyway."

During the few minutes it took to drive to Barnwold Farm, the stranger displayed considerable curiosity about Miss Melbourne's illness and Bart Wheeler's absence. The Dana girls were cautious, however, and gave him little information because there was something about this affected young man that aroused their instinctive distrust. It would be better, they reflected, to let him talk to Cousin Bessie.

Miss Marsh, however, did not receive the stranger with a great deal of enthusiasm.

"How do you do, Mr. Fayle?" she said, coolly.

"Call me Claude," he invited in a reproachful voice. "These charming young ladies tell me that Constance is ill, and that Bart is away."

"Yes, that's true. I'm afraid you won't be able to see either of them."

"Now that," declared Claude Fayle, "is most annoying. I had counted particularly on seeing Bart today. A little financial matter. I happen to be hard pressed for money just now—as a matter of fact, I'm *always* hard pressed for money—and I had looked to Bart to help me out. Really, I don't know what I'll do. When is he expected back?"

"I can't say," replied Miss Marsh.

Claude Fayle shook his head.

"Most annoying," he murmured. "I certainly need that money." Then, to the great astonishment of the Dana girls, he said calmly:

"If you happen to have a few dollars in your purse, my dear Bessie, perhaps you could accommodate me. I'm sure Bart will make it up to you when he comes back."

"I'm sorry," said Miss Marsh, "but I can't do that."

"Perhaps, then, your cousins—" hinted Claude Fayle.

"Quite impossible!"

Mr. Fayle sighed.

"Very well," he said. "Of course, a poor artist is accustomed to these rebuffs. The trouble with you Philistines is this: you place too much value on money. After all, what is money? Bits of metal—pieces of paper. All I ask of the world is enough to buy paints and brushes and canvas, just sufficient to advance my artistic career. But genius is never appreciated until it is dead. Good afternoon, Ladies."

He turned away abruptly and descended the walk, slashing viciously at the snow with his cane. Then he climbed into his car and drove in the direction of the Studio Tower.

"There," declared Bessie Marsh, "goes one of the laziest, most conceited and cheekiest persons who ever called himself an artist. Look at that hat! And the cape! And the cane! You would think he had just stepped out of a garret in the Latin Quarter. He has never been near France."

"Is he really a genius?" asked Louise.

"Genius!" scoffed Cousin Bessie. "Very far from being a genius. He can't paint, and he's too lazy to learn. He has been trying to win Miss Melbourne's favor through Bart, and is always borrowing money. I can't understand why Bart ever puts up with the fellow."

Jean, in the meantime, was watching Claude Fayle's car as it bumped and swerved down the road.

"Look!" she said suddenly. "He is stopping at the Studio Tower again."

"I hope he doesn't go in," said Bessie. "He knows Miss Melbourne is too ill to see anyone. But he wouldn't hesitate about asking her for a loan if she were dying."

Cousin Bessie's estimate of Claude Fayle's consummate impudence appeared to be correct, for the artist got out of his car and went directly up the path to the Tower.

"He's impossible!" breathed Bessie. "I hope Mammy Cleo shuts the door in his face."

Mammy Cleo did nothing of the kind. It was ten minutes before the Dana girls saw Claude Fayle emerge from the Studio Tower and hurry down the path toward the car.

"Louise," declared Jean, "I think he is carrying something under his coat."

"I'm sure of it. A big object, too. He seems to be trying to hide it."

"Perhaps he stole something."

"That," declared Louise, "is what we're going to find out. Come on."

The Dana girls hurried toward the Studio Tower. They had not reached the road, how-

ever, before they saw Claude Fayle's **car**
vanishing in the direction of Mount Pleasant.
It had disappeared by the time they reached the
Tower.  Hastening to the kitchen, they eagerly
questioned Mammy Cleo.

"Dat man wid de big hat?" exclaimed the
colored cook.  "He's jes' a nuisance, he is.
Come aroun' heah askin' 'bout Miss Constance.
I tol' him he better git away quick.  But he's
got de mos' nerb I ebber did see.  'I'll jes' wait
in de studio until de nu'se comes down,' he
says, an' he wait an' wait.  Den he go away."

"He wanted to borrow money from Cousin
Bessie," said Jean.  "You didn't give him anything, did you?"

"Me?" exclaimed Mammy Cleo, chuckling.
"You mus' think I'se sho' enough crazy.  Len'
money to him, an' you nebba sees it agin."

"But he took something away with him!"
cried Louise.

They ran into the studio.  One swift glance
proved their suspicion that Claude Fayle, although unsuccessful in his effort to borrow
money, had not departed empty-handed.  The
drapes that had hid the mysterious unsigned
portrait were drawn aside, revealing a blank
space beyond.

"The portrait has been stolen!" exclaimed
**Jean.**

# CHAPTER XI

## The Patient's Plea

Regardless of whether Claude Fayle had journeyed to the Studio Tower with the deliberate intention of stealing the picture, or whether the theft was merely the inspiration of a moment, he had been successful in his bold action. With a good fifteen minutes' start he was well on his way to a clear escape before the Dana girls could take up the chase.

With Mammy Cleo bewailing the loss of the portrait, fearing the grief of Miss Melbourne when she would learn of its disappearance, the Danas instantly went in pursuit of the thief. They borrowed a car from the garage and quickly set out on the artist's trail. Although they easily traced him as far as Mount Pleasant, they soon lost all track of the dilapidated roadster and its odd-looking passenger.

"Why did he steal one of Miss Melbourne's portraits, of all things?" exclaimed Cousin Bessie when the girls returned to Barnwold later and told her of the affair. "He couldn't possibly sell it as his own. Any dealer would recognize Miss Melbourne's signature."

"But the portrait wasn't signed," said Jean. Miss Marsh gasped.

"Surely it wasn't the hidden picture! Constance has been working at it for months." Bessie was greatly agitated. "She mustn't be told of this. The shock would kill her. I don't know the secret of that portrait, but I do know it has been a labor of love with her. She has always insisted that she could never be made to sell it or even exhibit it."

"Mammy Cleo was in a dreadful state when she learned it had been stolen," Louise ventured.

"No wonder. She realizes how precious the portrait is to Miss Melbourne."

This new development, transpiring in the very shadow of the tower, upset Miss Marsh a great deal. She pleaded with Jean and Louise to remain with her at Barnwold Farm a few days longer, explaining that she was so confused and bewildered by the succession of problems brought about by the disappearance of Josy, the flight of Bart Wheeler, the illness of Miss Melbourne, and the theft of the portrait, that she was unable to handle the situation alone.

"I do need your help," she told them. "I'm particularly eager to find Bart. He would come back, I'm sure, if he knew Constance was very ill."

The Dana girls wanted to do all in their power to help their cousin, but as they had given their promise that they would spend New Year's Eve with Uncle Ned and Aunt Harriet at Oak Falls, they could prolong their visit no later than the following day. Much as they disliked leaving Barnwold Farm with the mystery unsolved, yet they were forced to refuse Cousin Bessie's invitation.

They had hoped that Bart Wheeler would repent of his hasty departure and at least write a letter of explanation to Bessie. Next morning, however, when the postman called he brought no letter from Bart, nor was there any message from Josy Sykes.

"I'm *sure* she will write to us!" insisted Jean, fighting back her disappointment. "Perhaps she's just waiting until she gets settled—wherever she is."

They paid a farewell visit to the Studio Tower that afternoon. Mammy Cleo, who met them at the door, rolled her eyes warningly.

"Don' say nuffin' 'bout dat pitcher!" she cautioned the girls.

Then, to their surprise, she told them that they might see Miss Melbourne for a few minutes. They had not expected that they would be admitted to the sick room.

The patient, very pale and very weak, was no longer delirious, and recognized them at once. Her eyes brightened with an expression of gratitude.

"She is much better today," said the nurse in charge when the Dana girls glanced at her inquiringly. "Very ill yet, of course. She asked me to let you come up if you called."

Miss Melbourne's lips moved:

"Please," she whispered weakly, "please find Josy."

Again the girls were mystified by the great artist's concern for the crippled waif whom they had befriended.

"You must locate her for me," pleaded Constance Melbourne. "I'm so helpless, lying here—but she must be found——"

The nurse advanced toward the bed.

"You mustn't talk, Miss Melbourne," she cautioned. "Remember, you are very weak."

"May we ask her one question?" begged Jean. "Just one? Miss Melbourne, why are you so eager to find Josy?"

The woman merely shook her head and did not answer, so the Dana girls left the Studio Tower a few minutes later. Their bewilderment was as great as ever.

"Now why," asked Louise, as they halted in the shadow of the tower, "is the great Constance Melbourne so interested in Josy Sykes?"

Jean shook her head.

"It's beyond me," she admitted. "But we must find her."

The burden of the mystery had been placed definitely upon their slim shoulders, and it was a situation more difficult and more baffling than any they had yet encountered. There were no clues. Miss Melbourne was either unable or unwilling to give them an explanation of her anxiety for Josy's return. No letter had been received from either Josy or Bart Wheeler, so there was no apparent way of learning the fugitives' whereabouts.

When the Dana girls said goodbye to Cousin Bessie and returned to Oak Falls that night, it was with a dismal consciousness of failure. They were to return to Starhurst immediately after the New Year—and how could they ever hope to solve this mystery while there?

About a week later, while Louise and Jean were in their study at the school one evening, they suddenly became aware of a conversation which was being carried on in the hallway just outside their room.

"What happened to the little hunchback freak of the Danas?" Lettie Briggs was heard to ask.

"Lost her job, I was told " Ina Mason replied.

Lettie laughed shrilly.

"I always wondered how she ever got the job in the first place."

This conversation might have seemed casual, but in reality it had been carefully planned. Lettie and her chum were standing near the half-open doorway, well aware that the Danas could not help overhearing them.

"I wonder where they ever picked her up?" queried Ina with a malicious smile.

"It's a good thing she was dismissed. I was going to complain to my father and have him write to Mrs. Crandall," declared Lettie. "Imagine having a girl like *that* working in the school."

Inside the study Jean put down her book and rose halfway from her chair, her eyes blazing with anger. But Louise immediately restrained her.

"Shh!" she whispered. "They're doing it on purpose. Don't notice them."

Lettie and her chum waited expectantly in the corridor. They were fondly hoping that the Dana girls would rush out in anger, but nothing happened.

"Did you lock the door of my room when we came out?" asked Lettie.

"Oh, of course I did. I shouldn't think of leaving it unlocked. Someone might go in and discover our secret."

"And there are some girls in this school

who would give a lot to know that secret, too,"
declared Miss Briggs complacently.

"You're awfully clever to think of it,
Lettie."

"I guess there isn't anyone else at Starhurst
with a secret like it," came the boastful reply.

Lettie and Ina had hoped to annoy the Danas
and to arouse their curiosity, but there was
not a sound from the study. The two girls
finally sauntered away.

"The darlings!" muttered Jean ironically.

Louise laughed.

"They were trying to make us curious. They
would have been flattered if we had paid any
attention to them."

"Just the same," observed Jean, "I wish I
knew this great secret of theirs. The girls in
Lettie's own clique have been making mysterious visits to her study all week. I wonder
what it's all about."

"If you want to make Lettie Briggs feel
pleased with herself, just let it be known that
you're inquisitive about her secret," advised
Louise.

"Well, we have a secret, too," observed
Jean, "and I dare say Lettie is bursting to
know it."

"So we're square on that score," smiled
Louise. "She has her secret. We have ours."

Upon their return to the school Louise and

Jean had endured many veiled and malicious inquiries from Lettie Briggs regarding the whereabouts of Josy, but had given their snobbish schoolmate little satisfaction. Lettie, who had evidently made a New Year's resolution to be as disagreeable as possible for the remainder of the term, had gone out of her way to make herself unpleasant to the two Danas.

Moreover, she and the few girls in her set had spread vague hints throughout the school about a great "secret," the nature of which was wrapped in a mystery, that centered in Lettie's study. The Dana girls had pretended sublime indifference, and the little dialogue between Lettie and Ina had been staged outside their open door by way of tempting their curiosity. But Louise, shrewdly, had refused to be gullible.

When Lettie and Ina finally gave up the attempt and retreated down the corridor, Jean and Louise again bent over their books. Half an hour had passed when Jean suddenly raised her head, a puzzled frown on her face.

"Did you hear that, Louise?"

"I heard a whistling sound. It seemed to come from outside."

"Listen!"

A moment later the girls noticed a soft, peculiar whistle, vaguely familiar.

Jean went to the window and opened it.

The sound was repeated. Jean gazed at her sister in astonishment.

"Why, that's Josy's whistle!"

Both girls realized then why the odd notes had been so familiar. It was the weird, plaintive tune they had heard on the trail near Mohawk Lake the afternoon they had first met Josy Sykes.

Louise sprang to her feet.

"Perhaps she is outside signaling to us!" she cried.

The girls looked down from the window and out over the snow-covered campus. There was no one in sight, but their eyes could not penetrate the deep shadows cast by the school tower. As they listened, they heard the strange, familiar whistle again, clear and distinct on the frosty air.

"No one but Josy could do that!" declared Jean with finality. "I wonder if she is down there—in the shadow of the tower. Perhaps she needs us."

"We'll go outside," decided Louise practically.

When the girls slipped downstairs and hurried into the cold night, they found the campus deserted. There was no one in the shadow of the tower. They could not find even a footprint.

"I can't understand it," Jean said, puzzled.

# CHAPTER XII

## A Familiar Whistle

"I CAN'T understand it," Jean repeated. "We heard that whistle distinctly."

As if in mockery the strange notes again quavered through the air, but this time they seemed to come from overhead. When they died away, Louise and Jean stood staring at each other in amazement.

"I'm glad I'm not superstitious," said Louise. "Otherwise, I'd blame it on a ghost."

Jean looked up at the gloomy school tower, then at the high stone walls of the building. She could see the lighted windows of the studios above. Suddenly she snapped her fingers.

"I think I have it!" she exclaimed.

"What do you mean?" asked Louise.

"This is Lettie's big secret," answered Jean.

Without another word she turned and hastened back into the building, followed by the puzzled Louise who pleaded vainly for enlightenment. Jean led the way back toward their own study, then on down the corridor and up the stairs to the floor above. With a finger to her lips she cautioned for silence.

94

Lettie's room was but a few yards away.
Quietly the Dana girls crept down the hall.
At the closed door they paused. They could
hear faint sounds of scuffling in the study beyond, then Lettie's shrill, high-pitched giggle.

There followed a scrape, a squawk—and then
a man's voice:

" . . . and now we present Benny Blossom
and his Serenaders, playing a medley of the
latest hits from Broadway. . . ."

From beyond the door came the moan of a
saxophone, the beat of a drum, the piping notes
of a clarinet, the wail of a violin.

"A radio!" gasped Louise.

Jean nodded.

"That's the big secret," she whispered.

"Radios are forbidden at Starhurst," said
Jean.

The great mystery was solved. Lettie Briggs
and her chums, instead of devoting their evenings to study, were enjoying the privileges of
a radio which Lettie had somehow smuggled
into the school.

Jean and Louise retraced their steps as
quietly as they had come, and returned to their
study.

"But do you really think the whistling came
over the radio?" said Louise. "We didn't hear
music or an announcement either before or
afterwards."

"It was the fact that the whistling seemed to come from the air above us that gave me the hunch about the radio. If it was part of a program, it's strange we didn't hear more. Perhaps the whistling didn't come over the radio after all. It may have been one of the girls in Lettie's room."

"I'm disappointed," Louise confessed. "I was sure Josy Sykes was somewhere near."

"Just the same," said Jean, "I think if we are going to try to find Josy, we should follow every clue."

"You think we ought to make inquiry of the big broadcasting studios," added Louise, "to learn whether the girl we're trying to locate is on the air."

"Exactly," replied Jean.

Without delay the Danas penned identical letters to several broadcasting studios in the vicinity, asking the managers that if they were employing a hunchback named Josy Sykes, who whistled and sang, would they please give her a message. Would they tell her to get in touch with the Danas at Starhurst, as a very important matter had come up in regard to the health of someone who was asking for her. The letters were dispatched, although the girls had little hope that anything would come of them.

Jean's suggestion that the whistling might not have emanated from the radio after all was recalled to their minds next morning, for through the halls of Starhurst there trilled various renditions of that peculiar series of notes which were now so familiar to them. Lettie Briggs and her friends seemed to have developed a sudden interest in whistling.

"It's our clan call—a secret signal," proudly explained one giddy member of Lettie's crowd when a mystified sophomore sought an explanation.

"Not much of a secret about it," sniffed the sophomore. "I've heard that whistle twenty times this morning. Where did you learn it?"

"Oh, we can't tell that. It's part of our secret."

Lettie and her friends considered themselves very clever and original indeed, but the Danas were enjoying a little joke by themselves. Wouldn't the haughty Lettie be put out if she were to be told she was imitating something Josy Sykes could do?

There was a letter from Cousin Bessie in the morning mail, and the Dana girls dismissed Lettie's latest acquisition from their minds as they eagerly opened the missive. With every message from their relative they hoped for some news of Josy or Bart Wheeler, but invariably they were disappointed. This letter was like the others.

"We have had no word of Josy," it ran in

part, "and I am afraid we'll never hear of her again.

"I keep hoping that Bart will at least write to me, but so far there has not been a line. I have made inquiries in some of the artists' colonies, but none of his friends have heard from him. What could have made him drop out of sight like this?

"Miss Melbourne is still very ill, and her recovery is slow. She feels bad because she will not be able to have any work hung in the exhibition at Majestic this month——"

"Uncle Ned promised to take us to that exhibition," interrupted Louise.

Then Jean read on:

"She is particularly disappointed because she was working on a picture which she considered her masterpiece, and had hoped to finish it in time to display it at the exhibition. It will be a long while, however, before she will be able to resume work!"

The ringing of the bell for chapel suddenly interrupted their perusal of Bessie's letter, and the girls joined their scurrying schoolmates in the corridors. When the exercises were over that morning, the students were not immediately dismissed to their classrooms. Mrs. Crandall announced that she had a special notice.

"As many of you probably know," said the

headmistress, "we are soon to have the opportunity of viewing one of the finest exhibitions of the work of contemporary American artists. I refer, of course, to the forthcoming art exhibit in Majestic at the end of the month."

Mrs. Crandall paused, and looked out over the crowded chapel. Jean nudged Louise.

"A coincidence," she whispered. "Just what Cousin Bessie was writing about."

"I am very eager," continued the principal, "that the students of this school take advantage of this great opportunity. Majestic is not far enough away to prevent us from attending the exhibit. I plan to go myself, and Professor Crandall and I will chaperone a large number of the girls from Starhurst.

"The art students, of course, should be particularly interested. This morning we are being honored by a visit from one of our prominent American artists who will exhibit some of his latest works at the exhibition. He has kindly consented to address us for a few minutes and give a brief resumé of the pictures in the collection."

Mrs. Crandall appeared to be playing for time. There was no sign of any prominent painter on the platform, and she anxiously looked out over the chapel toward the doorway.

"We are very fortunate to have this noted

artist with us. He has, I may say, decided
to locate in Penfield for a time.'' The principal's face suddenly showed relief. ''Ah!''
she beamed. ''Here he is now.''

Down the aisle came an instructor, escorting
a stout, artistic-looking figure. The great
painter's hair was long, his clothes were worn
with studied carelessness, and his Windsor tie
fell in graceful folds.

Jean gripped her sister's arm. She craned
her neck, trying to get a glimpse of the artist's
face.

''Lou!'' she whispered, ''doesn't he remind
you of——?''

Just then the visiting lion reached the platform, turned around, and bowed.

''It gives me great pleasure,'' beamed Mrs.
Crandall, ''to introduce to you one of the
greatest of our younger American artists—Mr.
Claude Fayle.''

There, smirking upon the platform, stood the
man who had stolen Constance Melbourne's
mysterious painting!

# CHAPTER XIII

## THE IMPOSTOR

CLAUDE FAYLE, with consummate impudence, had succeeded in hoodwinking Mr. and Mrs. Crandall, and was now highly elated. Languidly playing the part of a great artist, he drawled and postured as he launched into a condescending address.

Louise and Jean were dumbfounded. Knowing Fayle to be an idle impostor, they were alternately amused and angry as he went on to tell his audience of the forthcoming exhibition, with special reference to his own work.

"I favor quality to quantity," drawled Mr. Fayle, running his fingers through his hair. "For that reason I have decided to exhibit but one of my new pictures at Majestic. It is, if I may be forgiven for saying so, one of my greatest efforts. So many of our modern artists turn out several paintings in such rapid succession that true beauty is lost and great art is impossible. I would rather spend years upon one great work than days upon a mediocre piece of no merit whatsoever."

His admiring audience applauded him vigorously. Mr. Fayle went on with a sketchy resumé of the other entries, but managed to convey the impression that they were inferior efforts and that his own solitary contribution would take all the honors of the show.

"Just wait," murmured Jean. "We'll make him sing another tune before long."

The girls could scarcely sit still long enough for Claude Fayle to conclude his talk, so eager were they to confront him and ask him what he had done with Miss Melbourne's portrait. But when the "great artist" had graciously bowed himself off the platform to the applause of his audience, he was immediately surrounded by a small group of gushing admirers, headed by Lettie Briggs.

"Oh, Mr. Fayle," cried Lettie, "this is one of the greatest moments of my life. I've heard so much about you. I've been simply dying to meet you. My daddy bought some of your beautiful paintings for the library at home."

Claude Fayle looked a trifle surprised at this announcement. To his certain knowledge no one had ever bought any of his paintings. However, he played up to Lettie's hero-worshipping antics, and was soon shaking hands with Ina Mason and other members of Lettie's crowd, gravely receiving their homage as if he had been accustomed to it all his life.

The Dana girls were unable to get past the outer fringe of the crowd. They could hear Lettie fawning on Claude Fayle.

"I'm something of an artist myself, you know," she was saying. "All my friends say I have real talent."

"Fancy that!" murmured Jean.

"You must let me paint your portrait, Miss Briggs," said Claude Fayle suavely. "Of course, I do very little portrait work, but when I find a really attractive subject——"

"Oh, Mr. Fayle!" giggled Lettie. "Do you honestly mean that? To think of having my portrait painted by the famous Claude Fayle!"

Lettie's chums raised an excited chorus. Mr. Fayle found himself so popular, with Lettie clinging to one arm and Ina to the other, that he made his way out of the chapel with difficulty. Jean and Louise had no opportunity of speaking to him, for a few minutes later the bell rang for classes.

However, they learned from gossip which Lettie managed to broadcast through Starhurst that morning that Claude Fayle was staying at the State Hotel, and planned to remain in Penfield for some time. This news served to relieve their disappointment in having failed to talk to the artist after chapel.

"We'll see him yet," declared Jean. "I think he'll not be very eager to talk to us."

"He certainly pulled the wool over Lettie's eyes. And the Crandalls seem to have taken him at face value."

It was through Lettie that the girls received definite information about Fayle's plans.

"I noticed that you were trying to get near enough to speak to my friend, Mr. Fayle, this morning," she said sweetly, encountering Jean and Louise in the lower hall after classes that afternoon.

Jean shrugged.

"We weren't really very eager," she replied. "We've met him before."

Lettie's face fell.

"Oh! Then perhaps you'll be interested to know that he is going to live in Penfield. He is moving into an apartment in Penfield Center tomorrow. I'm to see him at the hotel this afternoon about my sittings."

"Sittings?" said Louise politely.

"Yes. He's going to paint my portrait. Of course, he is tremendously expensive—a world-famous painter, and all that——"

"World-famous?" interjected Jean.

Lettie looked flustered.

"Well, Mrs. Crandall herself said he was famous."

"Strange," murmured Louise, "that I had never heard of him before Jean and I met him on our Christmas vacation."

"Well, anyway," snapped Lettie, "he is going to paint my portrait if I can persuade Daddy to let me have it done."

Thereupon she flounced away, evidently annoyed because the Dana girls gave no sign of being impressed.

In reality Jean and Louise were really much more interested than they appeared to be. If Claude Fayle was to live in Penfield, they would be able to do some detective work toward locating Miss Melbourne's painting. They were glad now that they had not spoken to the artist that morning, for he might have taken alarm at their presence.

"Let's go down to the hotel this afternoon after classes," Jean suggested. "If he is to meet Lettie there, we may be able to gather some information."

"Good idea. We'll go."

Thus it happened that when Lettie Briggs proudly entered the State Hotel late that afternoon and made her way across the lobby, two pairs of bright eyes were watching her. The Dana girls, ensconced behind a large palm, were eager witnesses to her arrival. Lettie went up to the desk, spoke to the clerk, then sauntered over to a comfortable chair where she languidly composed herself to wait—presumably for Claude Fayle.

Within a few minutes the artist stepped out

of the elevator. Jean and Louise, in the meantime, had found seats directly behind Lettie's chair. The high back shielded them from view.

"My dear Miss Briggs," breathed Claude Fayle soulfully, "it is so good of you to call."

"Oh, Mr. Fayle," gushed Lettie. "I'm simply thrilled. I've been so flattered to think that of all the girls at Starhurst you should have asked *me* to sit for my portrait."

"It is because your face has character, Miss Briggs. Beauty combined with character. You would make a marvellous subject for a portrait."

"He is certainly flattering her to the utmost," whispered Louise with disgust.

"Oh, Mr. Fayle," simpered Lettie, "I'm not really beautiful."

"Would I do you the honor of asking you to sit for your portrait if you weren't?" blandly replied Claude Fayle. "By the way, have you had any reply from your father?"

"I sent him a telegram today but I haven't had any answer yet. I wanted to ask you, Mr. Fayle—how much will it cost?"

"Cost?" said Claude Fayle. "Well, really, the matter of the fee is seldom mentioned. Most of my clients feel that the honor itself——"

"Oh, I do appreciate the honor!" said Lettie hastily. "But if I'm to have my portrait

done, Daddy will have to pay for it. He has
plenty of money, of course—I'm the wealthiest
girl at Starhurst—but he will want to know.''

"You understand that an artist of my reputation cannot afford to work for small prices.
I usually charge ten thousand dollars or more
for a single picture. However, I'm so eager
to transfer your beauty to canvas, Miss Briggs,
that we'll stipulate a nominal sum. Let's say
five thousand dollars.''

Lettie gasped. The Dana girls were dumbfounded. It was plainly evident that Claude
Fayle was playing on Lettie's vanity and ig-
norance with the object of making some easy
money, but the outrageous sum he had just
mentioned threw an unsavory light on the entire matter.

"It's a hold-up!'' whispered Jean indignantly.

"Nothing short of a confidence game,'' replied Louise. "We should warn Lettie.''

"Not now. She wouldn't believe us. Wait.''

Lettie Briggs had been momentarily staggered by Claude Fayle's cool assumption that
she could easily persuade her father to spend
five thousand dollars for her portrait. However, she tried to convey the impression that
the sum meant little to her.

"It's higher than I expected,'' she said.
"But of course, you cannot work for less.''

"Not a cent less," said Claude Fayle firmly. "As a matter of fact, several people in Penfield have asked me to accept commissions, but I have refused them. If I paint your portrait, it will take up much valuable time."

"Well," replied Lettie, getting up, "if I hear from Daddy tomorrow I'll let you know. Will you be here at the hotel?"

"I'm taking a studio in Penfield Center, at the Essex Apartments. You may telephone me there."

A few moments later Lettie Briggs departed from the lobby, and Claude Fayle returned to the elevator with a smile of extreme content-ment on his smug, self-satisfied face. It was a golden opportunity for the Dana girls to confront him and demand an explanation of the disappearance of Miss Melbourne's picture, but they decided to bide their time. It was a foregone conclusion that Fayle would deny ab-solutely any knowledge of the painting.

"We can't prove that he has it. We would just put him on his guard," Louise pointed out. "Our best plan is to watch him for a while."

"It's dishonest of him to charge Lettie's father five thousand dollars for a picture. We should expose him."

"If we were to go to Lettie and tell her that Fayle is a rascal, she wouldn't believe us. She would say we were jealous, and that would

make her more determined than ever. If she
really does go through with it and gets her
father's permission, we'll try to let him know,
in a friendly way, that he is being cheated."

Louise's wiser counsel prevailed, and the
girls took no immediate action toward blocking
the schemes of Claude Fayle. For the next
few days, however, they spent all their spare
time between classes watching the apartment
building where Fayle had taken up his quarters.

He was evidently making the most of his
opportunity. Heralded throughout Penfield as
one of the greatest artists of the day, he had
become something of a social lion. Inquisitive
people who wanted to know just where Fayle
earned his reputation and just what pictures
he had ever painted—if any—were condemned
as ignorant and uncultured. None of Claude
Fayle's admirers cared to admit that his name
was unknown to them before he appeared in
Penfield.

Mrs. Crandall, ordinarily a shrewd woman,
had made an error of judgment. She had introduced Claude Fayle to Penfield, and believed
in him implicitly. Even Mr. Crandall had become a regular visitor to the studio. The Dana
girls saw him entering or leaving the Essex
Apartments on a number of occasions.

Another caller, to their surprise, was their
friend, Mrs. Grantland, a wealthy Penfield

woman who had made the acquaintance of the girls when their clever detective work had resulted in the recovery of a stolen ring. The story of that affair has already been related in the first volume of this series, *By the Light of the Study Lamp.*

"That settles it," declared Louise firmly, when they discovered that the kindly, trusting Mrs. Grantland was evidently among Claude Fayle's prospective victims. "We're going to interview that young man."

"The sooner the better," agreed Jean. "He won't feel so sure of himself after we've talked to him."

Their decision to call on Claude Fayle demanded considerable courage. After all, they admitted they knew very little about the artist aside from what Cousin Bessie had told them. He was committing no crime by opening a studio in Penfield, and if people were foolish enough to pay exorbitant prices for his portraits Fayle was still within the law. As for Miss Melbourne's stolen picture, they were sure Fayle would flatly deny all knowledge of it. They would have to outwit him in some manner.

The following afternoon they watched the Essex Apartments for half an hour. After making sure that no one could see them, they went into the building, finding the number of

Claude Fayle's apartment readily by consulting the directory in the lobby. Then they ascended the stairs to the second floor.

The glass in the door of the studio bore the name of Claude Fayle in heavy black letters.

"Here's the place," said Jean.

With beating heart she rapped sharply on the glass.

"I hope he is alone," whispered Louise. They waited. There was no response.

Jean rapped again. After the third attempt they realized that they had made the errand in vain. Claude Fayle was not at home.

Jean stepped back and looked speculatively up at the open transom.

"Perhaps he saw us coming. Maybe he won't answer the knock."

"We'll soon find out," Louise declared. She spied a big packing box at the end of the hall. "Help me carry this, Jean," she called.

The two girls dragged and trundled the box down to the door, then upended it. Louise scrambled on top of the box. Her head was now on a level with the transom, and she leaned forward, peering into the apartment beyond.

"Careful!" cried Jean, as the box teetered alarmingly when Louise shifted her balance. "You'll fall."

She steadied the improvised ladder while Louise clung to the ledge above the door. A hasty survey of the studio showed that the place was deserted. Claude Fayle was not, as they had suspected, hiding from them.

Louise could see a large desk just within range of her bird's-eye view of the room, and craned her neck to get a better glimpse of the letters and papers scattered on the glass top.

Suddenly the box tilted beneath her weight.

"Look out!" cried Jean in alarm.

But the warning came too late.

Louise performed an undignified sort of dance step as she tried to maintain her balance. There was a moment of suspense—then the box toppled over.

A crash, a scream, a shriek, the shattering noise of broken glass, and Louise went hurtling to the floor!

## CHAPTER XIV

### A Valuable Clue

"Are you hurt?" cried Jean anxiously.

Louise sat up, a bewildered expression on her face. Thoughtfully she rubbed her elbow.

"No bones broken," she announced.

"But plenty of glass," said Jean ruefully.

In falling, Louise had been thrown against the glass front of the studio door. It had been shattered into a hundred pieces. They gazed solemnly at the havoc wrought. Louise scrambled to her feet.

"I'm glad Claude Fayle wasn't at home after all," she said.

"We'll have to see the janitor and pay for the damage," Jean suggested practically. "Perhaps he can set in a new glass before Mr. Fayle comes back."

"It will be just too bad if Claude Fayle should return now and find his window broken. Seeing that I'm to blame for it, I'll go and look for the janitor. I hope he won't be cross."

Louise, fortunately, had been unhurt by her fall, although it was a miracle that she had not been cut by the shattered fragments of glass. She hurried off toward the stairway, bent on locating the janitor of the apartments.

Jean, in the meantime, ventured over to the broken window. The jagged opening was sufficiently large to reveal the room beyond. She peered through the aperture in the faint hope that she might perhaps see Miss Melbourne's missing portrait in the studio.

The big desk caught her eye. Now, while the Dana girls enjoyed the details of their amateur detective work, they did not believe in methods that might be described as "sneaky," and Jean would have paid no attention to the letters that were lying open on the desk had it not been for one circumstance.

A name fairly leaped at her from a typewritten sheet not three feet away.

It was the signature of Bart Wheeler!

Jean pressed closer in her eagerness. She was justified, she felt, in scanning the letter to which Bart Wheeler's name was signed. It might hold some clue that would enable her to locate her cousin's fiancé.

The missive lay there in plain sight. It was brief and to the point. Jean read:

"My Dear Fayle: I'm sorry, but I can't let you have the loan you ask. The sum is greater than I can afford just now. However, since you say you are in actual

need, I am sending you ten dollars which
I hope will tide you over. I really can't
let you have any more.

Faithfully yours,

BART WHEELER."

Jean was disappointed. There was little to
interest her in this letter save the fact that
Claude Fayle was evidently in touch with
Wheeler. It occurred to her then that this
might be an old letter, written long before
Wheeler's disappearance. She looked at the
date line at the top of the sheet.

The letter had been typed the previous day.
Greatly to Jean's delight, this was followed by
an address: "No. 447 Park Street, Majestic."

Quickly extracting pencil and paper from her
handbag, Jean scribbled it down. Here, at last,
was a valuable clue. Bart Wheeler was living
in the city where the forthcoming art exhibit
was to be held. How Claude Fayle had learned
of his whereabouts she did not know.

"That wasn't such an unlucky accident after
all," remarked Jean, surveying the broken
window.

Louise returned in a few minutes with the
janitor, a fat, cheerful man who was not as
angry as they had feared he would be.

"Accidents will happen," he said philosophically. "As long as you pay for the broken

glass, I don't care. I guess Mr. Fayle will be sore, but I'll try to fix that up. Maybe I can get the glass put in there before he comes back.''

''We really didn't intend to do it!'' said Jean.

''Of course you didn't,'' grinned the janitor. ''People don't go around bustin' windows just for the fun of it.'' He began sweeping the fragments into a dustpan. ''Run along now and we won't say anything more about it.''

Relieved to have escaped the need of making embarrassing explanations as to how the window had actually been broken, the Dana girls paid the man, tipped him for his trouble, then hurried toward the stairs. They were just about to descend when they heard the sound of approaching footsteps from below.

They gazed down the rail. On the first landing they caught sight of a familiar figure. The white hair, the lanky, stooped figure, and mild face of Professor Crandall came into view.

''My goodness!'' gasped Louise. ''We mustn't let him find us here.''

They turned and hastily made their way back down the hall. If their instructor should encounter them in the building, he would certainly want to know the reason. The janitor looked up inquiringly as they approached.

''We're students at Starhurst,'' said Jean,

taking the man into their confidence. "Professor Crandall is just coming up the stairs, and we don't want him to find us here. Is there any other way out of the building?"

The janitor winked knowingly.

"The perfessor comes here quite often," he said. "I guess he'd make you stay in after school if he found you up here, eh?"

Professor Crandall's footsteps sounded on the second flight.

"Go down there to the end of the hall," whispered the janitor. "Quick, now! You'll find a stairway that'll take you to the back entrance."

Jean and Louise fled down the hall. They were none too soon. Hardly had their fluttering skirts vanished from view than Professor Crandall emerged onto the landing, beaming benevolently through his spectacles. He would not have looked so benign had he known that two of his pupils were even then scrambling hurriedly down the steps toward the rear of the building.

It had been a narrow escape. Yet another scare was in store for them. They had reached the ground floor and were hastening toward the tradesmen's entrance at the back when Jean suddenly grabbed Louise by the arm.

"Horrors!" she exclaimed. "Look who's coming."

Down the back alley sauntered none other than Claude Fayle, his cane dangling negligently over one wrist, Windsor tie flapping in the breeze, and broad-brimmed black hat tipped at a rakish angle. Why he had chosen to enter the building by the tradesmen's entrance was a mystery, but there he was, at the most inopportune time he could have chosen.

Jean and Louise had to act quickly. The door was open, but Claude Fayle, presumably deeply engrossed with problems of art, had not yet seen them. Jean dashed toward the basement steps, Louise close at her heels. They were not halfway down the flight before Claude Fayle ambled across the threshold.

Not daring to proceed further lest he be tempted to investigate should he hear the clatter of footfalls on the steps, they crouched down on the narrow stairs. Breathlessly they waited.

Claude Fayle reached the head of the basement steps. There he halted. The girls lived through a moment of suspense. Had he noticed them? Was he coming down the stairway, and would he see them?

Then they heard the scratch of a match. Claude Fayle had merely paused to light a cigarette. A moment later he went on toward the upper flight and ascended toward his apartment above.

Jean and Louise lost no time in making their escape from the building. Down the alley they fled until they reached one of the main avenues of Penfield. Then, at a more sedate pace, they turned their steps back toward Starhurst.

"We ran into nothing but hard luck that time," said Louise ruefully. "Everything went wrong that could go wrong."

"I shouldn't say that exactly," replied Jean. "What do you think of this?"

From her handbag she took the slip of paper on which she had written Bart Wheeler's address.

"Four forty-seven Park Street, Majestic," read Louise, mystified. "What does it mean?"

"It means that we've learned Bart Wheeler's address."

Louise was incredulous.

"But how?" she cried.

Jean then told her how she had spied the letter on Claude Fayle's desk through the opening in the shattered window.

"And so," she concluded, "I simply jotted down the address and here it is."

"We'll telephone to Cousin Bessie at once. Perhaps she can get in touch with him and persuade him to come back."

"Let's hope so."

When they returned to the school, they put through a long distance telephone call to Bessie Marsh at Barnwold Farm. When the answering voice came over the wire, Jean excitedly told her the good news.

"We've located Bart!" she cried. "Have you heard from him?"

"Where is he?" demanded Bessie, her voice trembling with emotion. "I haven't had any word from him since he left the Studio Tower."

"Well, he is in Majestic right now. At least he was there yesterday. This is the address."

"Wait a moment, Jean. I'll write it down."

Over the telephone Jean read to her the number and street of the house in Majestic.

"But how did you learn this?" asked Cousin Bessie.

"Oh, we've been doing a little detective work," Jean laughed. "Your old friend Claude Fayle is here in Penfield now. It seems that he learned where Bart is living, and was evidently trying to borrow some money. We got the address from a letter Bart wrote to him."

"And we have another clue," chimed in Louise, close beside the telephone. "We think we're on the trail of the portrait that was stolen from Miss Melbourne's studio."

"Oh, I do hope you find it. Has Claude Fayle the picture?"

"We don't know just yet, but we intend to find out."

"How is Miss Melbourne?" asked Jean.

An anxious note crept into Cousin Bessie's voice as she answered:

"She is very, very low. Her condition is critical. And she has been asking for you. Could you possibly come to see her? She says there is something she wishes to tell you."

"We might be able to go this week-end. To-day is Friday. Tomorrow, perhaps."

"Come as soon as possible," urged their cousin. "If you delay—it may be too late."

"Is it that serious?" cried Jean in consternation. "I thought she was making a good recovery."

"She had a relapse. As a matter of fact," said Bessie, with a catch in her voice, "I doubt if she will recover."

"We'll come, then," decided Louise quickly. "We'll get permission from Mrs. Crandall tonight and leave here as soon as possible tomorrow."

"Please do."

The Dana girls were deeply concerned by their cousin's bad news. The gravity of her voice indicated that she held out very little hope for Miss Melbourne. Instantly they began making arrangements for a hurried visit to Barnwold Farm.

"But I can't imagine why Miss Melbourne was asking for us," declared Jean.

"And what can she want to tell us?"

They were soon to know. From their visit to Constance Melbourne's sickbed they were to learn much that was to throw a new and strange light upon the series of mystifying events that had begun with their encounter of Josy Sykes. What they were to hear was destined to emphasize the urgency of solving the riddle, not alone for Josy's sake, but for Constance Melbourne's as well.

# CHAPTER XV

## MISS MELBOURNE'S STORY

DISTURBED and excited over this serious turn of events, Jean and Louise could scarcely sleep that night. They readily obtained permission from Mrs. Crandall to spend the week-end at Barnwold Farm when they had explained the circumstances. Saturday afternoon found them hastening up the steps of the Studio Tower.

They had paid a brief visit to Barnwold, where Cousin Bessie told them that scant hope was held out for Miss Melbourne's recovery. There were tears in her eyes when she related how the great artist had suffered a serious relapse and had grown gradually weaker.

"She has asked for you continually in the past few days," said Cousin Bessie, "and is afraid she is going to die. There is something she wishes to tell you before it's too late."

At the Studio Tower the Dana girls entered an atmosphere tense and gloomy. Mammy Cleo, who met them at the door, was overcome with grief.

"Jes' as soon as dat picture went out of dis place," declared the old woman, "Ah knowed bad luck was bound to come. And it wuz all mah fault."

Dabbing at her eyes with her apron, the colored woman led the girls up the winding stairs to Constance Melbourne's room. A nurse met them at the door.

"The Dana girls?" she asked softly. "Come in, please. I'm glad you are here. Miss Melbourne has been asking for you."

Quietly they entered the sickroom. The shades were drawn, but they could distinguish the thin, pale face of Miss Melbourne. It was obvious that she was critically ill. Her eyes lit up a trifle, however, when she recognized her visitors.

"I've been hoping and praying that you would come," she said weakly. "Please sit down."

With a feeble gesture she dismissed the nurse from the room.

"I have something very important to tell these girls," she explained. "It may be my last opportunity."

She bade them to be seated, one at either side of the bed. Her wasted hands groped for theirs as if she sought to gather strength and confidence from them.

"I want to tell you about Josy Sykes," said

Miss Melbourne in a voice that was little more than a whisper. "You haven't found her yet, I suppose?"

"We have done our best, Miss Melbourne," said Jean. "But no—we haven't found her."

"I shall never see her again. Never in this life."

Her voice was filled with such unutterable pathos and remorse that the girls were touched. They were deeply sorry for Miss Melbourne. At the same time they could not help but wonder what tragedy lay behind her words. What deep mystery was shadowing her life? In what manner had the threads of her destiny become entangled with those of the crippled Josy Sykes?

"No doubt you have been puzzled about my interest in the child," continued the sick woman, sensing their unspoken thought. "I should have told this story before now. But —I—I had hoped—that I would get better—and make restitution."

Her voice was trembling with emotion.

"I have a confession—a terrible confession —to make."

The effort of speaking had sapped her strength, and she was obliged to rest. It was several minutes before she was able to continue.

"Years ago," went on Miss Melbourne,

"when I was a girl of eighteen, a boy fell in love with me. He was a poor boy. He worked on his brother's farm and had very little education—but he loved me."

Miss Melbourne gazed into space as the memory of that romance of long ago returned to haunt her mind.

"My parents were wealthy," she said. "I had every advantage that money could buy. Joseph was poor, but he was not so poor that he couldn't express his devotion to me. He wrote me poems, the only poems that anyone has ever written to me. He wrote them as if I were a princess."

A faint smile crossed her white, thin face.

"It was a long time before I realized that I cared for him. He worked hard, saved up enough money to give himself a fair education, and did everything to improve himself. When I knew him better, I respected him and finally fell in love with him. Poor Joseph! He wanted to marry me."

"And you refused?" whispered Louise in solemn wonder.

"It was so hopeless," sighed Miss Melbourne. "Our positions in life were far apart. My parents objected and said I must not see him any more. So—I had to send him away."

Miss Melbourne closed her eyes as if in pain at the recollection. The two girls then felt something of the tragedy that had shadowed the life of this great artist whom they had envied as one who had been given all that life could offer.

"Joseph," continued the sick woman wearily, "lived with his older brother. This brother was married to a charming woman, and they had one little girl. She had been named after her uncle and was called Josephine."

Jean and Louise looked at each other, startled. They began to glean some inkling of the truth.

"In time, I think," went on Miss Melbourne, "Joseph might have made his way in the world. I was content to wait, for I had faith in him and I believed he would eventually overcome my parents' objections to our marriage. But a dreadful tragedy intervened."

Her voice was hushed.

"The brother and his wife were killed in a railroad accident. The little girl was left an orphan."

"How dreadful!" murmured Jean.

"The child was alone in the world, except for her uncle. Joseph was all she had. And he felt that it was his duty to devote his life to her."

"And the child—?" exclaimed Louise eagerly.

"The child," said Miss Melbourne, her

voice deep with sadness, "was Josephine Sykes."

Silence hung over the sickroom. So amazed were the girls they dared not venture to speak. Now they knew why Miss Melbourne had been so concerned when she learned Josy's name.

"Joseph," continued Miss Melbourne, "was a brave and unselfish man. His true depth of character was revealed when he faced the fact that he had been left with this motherless child in his care. He did not shrink from his duty. He gave up all his hopes of a career, his dreams of a college education, and his ambition to fight his way to a commanding place in the world. To him, the child came first. He accordingly settled down on the farm and put out of his mind all thought of ever marrying me."

Miss Melbourne's eyes were wet with tears.

"I think I loved and respected him more then than ever. But what could I do under the circumstances? He was only a poor farmer and would never rise above his lot in life. I saw that I would have to put him out of my heart. I went to Europe, traveled, studied, and tried to forget. In time I became engaged to a brilliant singer, a young man who was approved by my parents. It would have been an ideal marriage—but for one thing."

"And what was that?" asked Jean.

"I didn't love him," returned Miss Melbourne simply. "I didn't love him, and as the day for the wedding drew nearer I knew in my heart that I should never be happy. One day I slipped away to the old farm to see Joseph, the man whom I really loved."

The sick woman was beginning to feel the strain of her prolonged effort. Feverish flecks of color appeared in her cheeks, but she was determined to finish.

"I adored Josy, the baby. She was only a little tot, and when I picked her up and held her in my arms I felt that my place was not in the outside world at all, but right there on that shabby little farm. I was happy there. Oh, if I could have known the consequences of that visit!

"I had picked Josy up and was carrying her about, singing with happiness. The dear child was laughing and crowing in my arms. To this day I do not know exactly how it happened— but I made a misstep, and stumbled and fell right on the brink of an old well-hole. The baby and I plunged many feet to the bottom."

The girls shuddered.

"I wasn't badly hurt," continued Miss Melbourne, wretchedly, "but as for Josy—from that day to this she has been a hopeless cripple —a hunchback."

Tears filled her eyes, and she broke down and sobbed uncontrollably at the recollection of the terrible accident. Jean and Louise pitied the stricken woman from the depths of their hearts. Gently they tried to soothe her with their sympathetic words, and at last Miss Melbourne became calmer.

"There is little more to tell," she said. "I know Joseph realized it was an accident. I would give anything in the world to retrace the awful step that blighted the poor child's life. Joseph had lost me and now I had brought sorrow and suffering into the life of the only other human being he had in the world. He was utterly heartbroken. I suppose he didn't mean to be unkind, but when I recovered from the effects of the fall I found that he had disappeared. He had sold the farm, packed up quietly, and fled with Josy. I have never seen him since."

Miss Melbourne gestured limply.

"That is my confession," she said. "Now you know why I must find Josy. I have never been able to make restitution to her for the terrible wrong I have done. It was an accident, of course, but my life since that time has been shadowed by the knowledge that while I was enjoying wealth and success and fame—that poor child might be enduring poverty and hardship. Before I die, I want to make restitution to her and to her uncle, if they can be found.

"After the accident I postponed my wedding

and finally broke my engagement. I spent much
time and money trying to locate Joseph and the
crippled baby, but not until you brought that
poor child to Barnwold Farm with you have I
had the slightest clue.''

This, then, was Miss Melbourne's secret. A
black thread of tragedy had wound itself about
three lives, and now one of those lives hung in
the balance. The mystery upon which the Dana
girls had stumbled assumed gigantic propor-
tions. It was vitally important now that Josy
Sykes should be found.

"I had a photograph of Joseph Sykes," went
on Miss Melbourne. "It was a picture of him
as he was in the days when I knew him as a
young man. I have treasured it for years. He
is greatly changed now, I suppose, but his
image will always live in my heart as he was
then.

"For a long, long while I have devoted myself to painting a portrait of him. Into that
picture I have put all the feeling and skill I
possess. When I felt sad or lonely, it comforted me to work on it, for it always brought
back so many memories. Most of them were
unhappy ones, it is true, but there were brighter
recollections as well—memories of the old farm
and of my own girlhood, of Joseph's little
poems, our hopes and dreams——"

Her voice choked. She could not go on.

Then she relaxed her grasp of Jean's hand and reached toward a silken cord hanging beside the bed and tugged at it feebly.

Far off down in the Studio Tower the girls heard the distant note of a bell.

Wondering, they waited. Miss Melbourne lay with closed eyes, overcome with exhaustion. Then came shuffling footsteps in the corridor, and a moment later the massive figure of Mammy Cleo appeared in the doorway.

"Yo' want me, Miss Constance?" asked the old woman humbly.

"Yes, Mammy Cleo," replied Miss Melbourne in a weak voice. "I want you to bring me something from the studio."

Mammy Cleo looked frightened. She rolled her eyes and glanced nervously at the girls.

"What yo' want ole Mammy Cleo to bring you, Miss Constance?" she asked.

"You know that picture behind the drapery? The portrait upon which I've been working for such a long time? The 'sad picture'? Please bring it to me, Mammy Cleo. I want these girls to see the picture of Joseph Sykes."

Jean and Louise were overwhelmed with dismay. What would be the effect upon Miss Melbourne when she learned that the portrait had been stolen?

# CHAPTER XVI

## The Shadow Beneath the Tower

The Dana girls were pale with apprehension when they heard the invalid ask for the stolen portrait. Miss Melbourne had never been told of its loss. The shock might prove fatal if she were to learn of its disappearance now. But what could they say? What could they do?

Mammy Cleo shook with fear.

"Sho', Miss Constance," she said. "Yo' don't want dat big pitcher brung 'way up here, does yo'? De gals can see it easy 'nuff when dey go down."

"But I want it, Mammy Cleo," pleaded Miss Melbourne. "I want it right here in my room. Go, now, and get the portrait. Please."

Mammy Cleo backed away, mumbling to herself, and throwing an appealing glance at the girls.

"Please turn on the lights," whispered Miss Melbourne.

Time had passed swiftly. So deeply engrossed were the girls in the invalid's story that they had scarcely noticed that darkness had fallen and that the room was now shrouded

133

in shadow, broken only by the light from the hall.

"Perhaps," ventured Louise, "we have excited you too much, Miss Melbourne. It has been a very great strain. We should go now."

"No, you must see the portrait! Please! I am so proud of it. Mammy Cleo will bring it up in a few minutes."

The girls did not dare break the news to her, for the risk was too great. But they realized that unless something happened to save the situation, Mammy Cleo would be forced to confess that the treasured picture was no longer in the studio. In their minds they bitterly condemned that unscrupulous rascal, Claude Fayle.

Through the house there suddenly floated a haunting strain of music. The notes of an old-fashioned waltz rang through the corridors and echoed from the walls of the tower. Somewhere an orchestra was playing, sweetly and softly.

Miss Melbourne smiled.

"It's the radio," she said. "The nurse has just turned it on. They won't allow me to have it in my room."

The melody continued with rising volume. The sweet music seemed to give the invalid pleasure, for she lay with a sad smile on her face, listening as if entranced. Finally the strains died away. There was a moment of silence.

Then, clearly and distinctly on the night air, the girls heard a peculiar whistle.

They sat up, tense and eager. It was the same whistle they had heard on the trail from Mohawk Lake, the whistle they had heard from Josy Sykes, the whistle they had heard while in their study at Starhurst. There was no mistaking the peculiar trill, the strange, haunting resonance, the weird musical notes.

"The radio is very clear tonight," murmured Miss Melbourne.

Jean rose from her chair. She was very pale. That whistling, she was convinced, could have been created by no one but Josy Sykes. Although the girls had received no reply from their letters to the broadcasting companies, they had not yet given up hope that they would find her by that method. Perhaps they had not been in touch with the right stations.

"Please excuse me, Miss Melbourne," she said. "I should like to speak to Miss Robertson for a moment."

She hastened from the room. It had struck Jean that this time she would get an explanation of the whole matter. The time she had heard the same tune before, she had not known what program might have contained the whistling. Now she would be able to trace the source of the entertainment and thus surely locate the missing girl.

A light indicated the nurse's room at the end of the corridor. Hastily Jean entered.

"Nurse!" she cried in excitement. "Tell me what station that program is coming from."

Nurse Robertson, who was sitting at the table examining a chart, looked up in surprise.

"Program?" she exclaimed. "What do you mean?"

Jean gestured toward the radio.

"The radio program. The whistling."

"But I just turned off the radio a few minutes ago," replied the nurse.

Jean was stunned. She had heard the whistling as she ran down the hall, but now the sound had died away. And the radio, as Miss Robertson had said, was not now in operation.

"I turned it off after that waltz number," explained the nurse. "It seems to me that I did hear someone whistling, but I didn't pay much attention to it. Certainly it didn't come over the radio."

Completely bewildered, Jean left the room. She had been so convinced that her theory was correct that the most obvious explanation eluded her altogether. Slowly she descended the winding staircase of the Studio Tower.

The silence was suddenly broken by a wild, terrified scream. It rang through the building, a yell of sheer fright. Then Mammy Cleo came running across the studio floor, wringing her hands and babbling with fear.

Jean ran down the few remaining steps.

"Mammy Cleo!" she cried. "What is it? What has frightened you?"

The colored woman clung to Jean for protection. She moaned with terror and pointed a trembling finger toward one of the huge studio windows.

"Ah knowed it!" she said. "Ah knowed it. 'Twuz all mah fault dat de pitcher was stole. An' now Ah's haunted."

"Nonsense!" Jean assured her. "What have you seen?"

"A ghos'," declared Mammy Cleo. "Big, black ghos' out in de snow." She began to shudder and groan. "Big ghos' come to haunt me 'cause Ah let dat pitcher git stole."

Louise, alarmed by the outcry, had left Miss Melbourne's room and hurried down the staircase.

"Ghost?" she cried, coming up to Mammy Cleo. "There are no ghosts, Mammy, and you know it."

But the old woman, groaning and shaking her head, again pointed to the studio window.

"Dey *is!*" she insisted. "You go look out

dat window. Bigges' black ghos' Ah ever did see. Ohhh! I'se scairt.''

Jean walked over to the window and drew the heavy curtains aside. Louise, at her shoulder, gazed out into the courtyard beneath the tower.

It was a clear moonlight night and the snow was as white as paper, in startling contrast to the black walls and heavy shadows. In the velvet sky there twinkled a million stars, and the moon was a plaque of dazzling silver. The brilliant illumination revealed every detail of the snow-covered courtyard.

As the girls watched breathlessly, they saw a strange figure emerge from the shadow of the tower. At the same time, upon the wall in the moonlight, there appeared a weird and hideous shadow. When the figure moved, the shadow moved. It was enormous and distorted, like some terrifying goblin with immense arms and a hunched back.

Mammy Cleo, recovering a little from her fright, had cautiously approached the window. Yet when she saw that grotesque shadow on the wall of the tower, she flung her apron over her head and sank down in the nearest chair, groaning with terror.

"See dat!" she cried. "See dat! You say dey's no ghosts now?''

The girls had been rendered speechless with

amazement, but still they were not frightened. They knew the origin of that hideous shadow, and it seemed to them like an answer to prayer.

"Josy Sykes!" breathed Jean in awe.

They saw the crippled figure advance into the courtyard with faltering, awkward footsteps. It was indeed Josy Sykes.

Louise ran to the door and flung it open. The warm light of the studio fell in a brilliant patch on the snow outside, revealing the pale face and wide eyes of Josy as she stood there, apparently afraid to advance any nearer the threshold.

Mammy Cleo emitted an ear-splitting scream. "Go 'way! Go 'way, ghos'," she cried. "Come to haunt me, 'cause Ah let dat pitcher git stole. Go 'way!"

Josy shrank back. She was so sensitive to the effect her deformed appearance might have upon other people that Mammy Cleo's wild cry struck her like a physical blow. She turned her head from the light that streamed through the open door, and might have stumbled away into darkness again had not Louise sprung across the threshold.

"Josy!"

When she heard the warm, eager voice of her friend, poor Josy wheeled about, a smile of indescribable joy on her pathetic face. She held out her arms, and a moment later Louise had enveloped her in a loving embrace. Then Jean hurried out, wild with delight. Thus it happened that in the shadow of the tower Josy was restored to her dearest friends.

"I'm so glad to come back to you," sobbed Josy, her eyes filled with tears of happiness. "Oh, it's so good to be with you again."

"It's so wonderful to have you here, Josy!" cried Louise. "You could not have come at a better time."

"You got our message?" asked Jean.

"Yes," replied Josy, "but how did you ever find out where I was?"

"Never mind that now," said Louise quickly. "We have some important news for you."

Josy was puzzled.

"I—I thought you would be glad to see me," she said, "although I acted so disgracefully in running away. But what do you mean by saying that I could not have come at a better time, and that you have important news for me?" the girl questioned wonderingly.

Louise held the crippled girl closer to her.

"We have a wonderful secret to tell you," she said.

# CHAPTER XVII

## An Emergency Call

"A secret?" cried Josy.

"Yes, indeed," declared Jean. "It clears up so many things that have puzzled us."

"And it concerns you," Louise added. "You and your uncle Joseph."

Josy was perplexed.

"But how can you possibly know anything about my uncle?" she demanded. "You have never seen him. I scarcely mentioned him to either of you."

"Josy," asked Louise gravely, "did your uncle ever tell you how you came to be crippled?"

Josy shook her head.

"He would never tell me. I only know that I was not born deformed. It—it happened in some sort of accident."

"Then we'll begin at the beginning. Do you know that Miss Melbourne has been dangerously ill?"

"I didn't know," admitted Josy. "Is that why you are here? I tried to find you at Starhurst, but they said you were spending the

week-end at Barnwold Farm, so I came out
here. But your Cousin Bessie was not at
home—the housekeeper said she had taken the
late train for Majestic and that you had come
here. So I followed.''

"Miss Melbourne has been very, very ill
ever since the night you went away from Barnwold Farm," explained Louise. "She has
asked for you constantly, and today she sent
for us. We have just come from her bedside
after hearing the strangest kind of a story.
Josy, there is no time to lose. You must go to
her at once. She needs you. She wants to
see you."

"But why?" demanded Josy in amazement.
"I don't know Miss Melbourne. Why should
she have any interest in me?"

"Because she knew you when you were a
baby!"

Poor Josy could make neither head nor tail
out of these disconnected revelations. Nevertheless, she listened patiently and with growing wonderment as the girls told the story of
Joseph Sykes as Miss Melbourne had related
it to them. She sobbed pitifully when they related Miss Melbourne's grief-stricken account
of the accident that had crippled her for life.

"Uncle Joseph would never tell me," she
said. "It's the first time I have ever known
how it happened."

"She has gone all these years hoping to ask your forgiveness, and now feels that it will soon be too late. She is very ill, Josy, and does not think she will ever get better again. She wanted us to find you so that she could make some restitution."

"Restitution!" exclaimed Josy. "But I don't want anything. It was an accident. She must have suffered terribly. If I can see her, I'll be only too glad to let her know that I hold nothing against her and that she has my forgiveness."

The true nobility of Josy's character was shown by her eagerness to alleviate the sick woman's distress. She could hear the truth about the terrible stigma that had followed her through life, yet could think of the woman who had unwittingly caused it without the slightest trace of resentment or hostility. There was no thought in her mind now but to hasten to Miss Melbourne's bedside and assure the invalid of her forgiveness and friendliness.

While the three girls were standing in the shadow of the tower, they saw the headlights of an approaching automobile swinging in from the Mount Pleasant road. The car was traveling at a high rate of speed and drew to a sudden stop, with a grinding of brakes, before the Studio Tower.

Two men leaped out and ran up the path toward the door. At the top of the steps they were met by Nurse Robertson. By the light that shone over the entrance, the Dana girls recognized one of the visitors as Miss Melbourne's physician.

"I hurried out the moment I got your 'phone call, Miss Robertson," exclaimed the physician. "Very fortunately Dr. Derwent, the heart specialist, was with me at the time, so I asked him to come along too. What is the trouble?"

"It's very urgent, Doctor," replied Miss Robertson. "The patient has taken a sudden turn for the worse. I'm afraid it is the end."

The shocked listeners heard no more as the two medical men vanished quickly across the threshold, closing the door behind them.

"She is sinking!" gasped Louise, her face white with anxiety.

Jean seized Josy by the hand.

"Come! We must hurry!"

They ran through the snow, hastened up the steps, and opened the door. Standing in the Studio Tower they could see the doctor and the specialist hurrying up the winding stairs, followed closely by the nurse. When they reached the gallery that overlooked the studio, they quickly made their way to Miss Melbourne's room, flinging aside their wraps. Every gesture betokened anxious haste. A moment later, Mammy Cleo, who had been left with the patient while the doctors were being admitted, emerged from the sickroom and descended the staircase, weeping audibly. When she reached the bottom, the old servant crumpled up in a heap, her hands clasped in prayer.

"Oh, Lawd!" she moaned. "Please don' take mah Miss Constance away. Please, Lawd, let her git well again. Dis ole cullud woman cain't git along widout her nohow. She's been mighty sick, Lawd, but she's jes' got to git well again."

Sobbing with grief, the faithful old woman uttered her heartbroken appeal. Miss Robertson suddenly appeared on the staircase, hurrying down toward the kitchen. Her face was serious.

"What has happened, Nurse?" asked Louise quickly.

"She has had a very sudden relapse," whispered Miss Robertson. "She is sinking rapidly. I'm afraid there is no hope."

She ran on to the kitchen.

Josy looked appealingly at the Dana girls. "I came too late!"

"No!" declared Jean. "It isn't too late. There is still time. You must see her. She must know that she has your forgiveness."

Seizing Josy by the hand, she made her way toward the staircase. Louise, realizing that the climb would tax the cripple's strength, put

her arm around Josy's waist. They began the
ascent toward the sickroom.

Never would they forget that tortuous journey as they helped Josy Sykes up the winding
flight of stairs. They were haunted by the fear
that the shadow of death might even then have
passed over the tower; they were oppressed
by the thought that Miss Melbourne might be
unconscious and unable to realize that her last
wish had been granted.

At last they came within sight of the sickroom. While they were still a few yards away,
however, the doctor moved swiftly from the
patient's bedside and closed the door. Josy
shook her head, stricken with disappointment.

"They won't let me see her!"

"They shall!" declared Jean impetuously.
She knocked gently at the door.

For a moment there was no response. Then,
very slowly, the door opened. They saw the
grave face and serious eyes of the doctor.

"Please," begged Josy, "I must see her.
She has been asking for me."

The doctor shook his head.

"I cannot allow it," he said. "Miss Melbourne is sinking rapidly. There will be a
definite crisis within a few minutes."

"Isn't there any hope?" pleaded Louise.

"None," he replied.

"She is still conscious?"

"Yes—but in a few minutes now—I am afraid—if she sinks into a coma it will all be over."

"Then," declared Jean with finality, "you must let Josy see her while there is still time. It means more to Miss Melbourne than you can imagine."

Their anxious faces and Jean's determined words impressed the doctor. He hesitated for a moment, then stood aside.

"Very well," he said.

Slowly the three girls filed into the sickroom where Miss Melbourne lay fighting her battle for life.

# CHAPTER XVIII

## The Danas' Discovery

The great specialist who was in attendance at Miss Melbourne's bedside frowned and shook his head in disapproval, as the three girls came into the room. He did not favor the intrusion.

Miss Melbourne stirred restlessly. Then she opened her eyes.

"Who is it?" she whispered.

Jean and Louise did not advance more than a few steps beyond the door.

"Go to her quickly," whispered Louise to the crippled girl.

Josy Sykes crossed the room, and moved toward the bed with faltering steps. Miss Melbourne's large gray eyes were fixed steadily upon her.

"Who are you?" whispered the invalid.

Josy leaned over the side of the bed, caught up the thin, wasted hand and pressed it to her lips.

"I am Josy!" she said.

There was a cry of joy from Miss Melbourne. It was a cry that seemed to tax her fading strength, for she lay back among the pillows and closed her eyes. A faint smile of happiness crept about the corners of her mouth.

"Josy?" she whispered at last. "You are really Josy Sykes?"

"Yes."

"I have tried to find you—for such a long, long time. I have done you a great wrong, Josy——"

Josy leaned forward, shaking her head.

"Shh! You must not speak. I came to tell you that I forgive you if there is anything to forgive. But I know you were not to blame. You must get better quickly so that we may be friends."

"I shall never get better, Josy. I wanted to find you, to make restitution to you and your uncle——"

Josy silenced her firmly.

"You mustn't speak like that, Miss Melbourne. My uncle never bore you any ill will. As for me, I was never told how I became a cripple. You aren't going to die."

"Ah, Josy, merely to know that you forgive me for the dreadful burden I placed on your life gives me some strength."

"For my sake, you must try to get well again."

"For your sake, Josy."

Miss Melbourne's eyes closed. Jean and

Louise had drawn back toward the door. Josy turned and tiptoed away from the bed, her eyes wet with tears. Together the girls left the room. Once out of Miss Melbourne's presence, Josy broke down and wept uncontrollably.

"Oh, she must not die! She must not die!" sobbed the crippled girl.

They went downstairs into the studio sitting room. The door of the sickroom had closed again. They sat talking in whispers, tense and anxious. They saw Nurse Robertson returning upstairs. They could hear Mammy Cleo praying audibly in the kitchen.

As the big clock in the studio solemnly ticked the seconds away, the girls wondered what was happening beyond the grim and impassive door of the patient's room.

"If the worst comes to the worst," said Louise quietly, holding Josy's hand, "you have at least set her mind at rest."

Finally, after long minutes had passed, the door of the sickroom opened and the nurse emerged. Her crisp white uniform rustled as she quickly descended the staircase. When she hurried over to the girls, they saw that her eyes were shining.

"It's a miracle!" she breathed. "Nothing but a miracle!"

"Is she getting better?" cried Jean eagerly.

"She has rallied. Just when the doctors had

given up all hope, too. She has passed the crisis and now is resting easier.''

''Oh, thank goodness!'' Josy cried, her voice tremulous with relief.

''It was your visit that did it,'' declared the nurse. ''Whatever you said to her seemed to give her new strength. Up to that time she had been discouraged and ready to give in. Then she began to fight against the weakness. She'll recover now, I'm sure.''

Suddenly the nurse looked sharply at Josy.

''Why, you're Josy Sykes, aren't you?''

''You remember me, Miss Robertson?''

''Indeed I do. I was head nurse at the Home for Crippled Children when you were there. The Dana girls were speaking to me about you just the other day. Josy, child, you were a foolish girl to leave the Home when you did,'' the nurse reproved gently.

''I couldn't stay, Miss Robertson. I knew they suspected me of stealing that money, but I didn't do it. Really I didn't.''

''My dear child, nearly all of us were quite sure you were innocent, but you didn't improve your position by running away.''

''It—it was because I got a large sum of money in a letter. I knew that if anyone learned that I had the money, they might think I had really taken the benefit receipts.''

''The truth will come out some day, Josy.

And when the truth is known I think we'll discover that Mrs. Rita Rye took that money.''

"Mrs. Rye!" exclaimed Josy in amazement. "But she is one of the trustees.''

"Trustee or no trustee—she had access to that money as well as need of it. I happen to know that she was head over heels in debt, even with all her fine clothes and her haughty manners. You mark my words, Josy, she knows what happened to the money.''

"If we could only prove it, and thereby clear Josy's name!'' exclaimed Jean.

"Will you help me?'' asked the cripple eagerly.

"Of course we'll help,'' Louise declared.

"You'll have your work cut out for you,'' said the nurse. "It's quite a while since the money was stolen. Still, if you do try to solve the case I'd advise you to concentrate on Mrs. Rita Rye.''

The door of the sickroom opened just then and the specialist, a stout, elderly man with shrewd eyes and a close-clipped mustache, came down the stairs. As he approached the little group they saw that he was smiling.

"You may go home now, if you wish,'' he said. "There is no danger. Miss Melbourne will recover. It's been nothing short of a miracle.''

"Is she resting easier?'' asked Louise.

"She fell into a natural sleep. She rallied in the nick of time. Before this young lady spoke to her," and he indicated Josy, "it was my opinion that she had no more than a few minutes to live."

The girls were overjoyed. Their first impulse was to go at once to Barnwold Farm and tell Cousin Bessie the good news. They hurriedly donned their wraps, and after bidding good night to Miss Robertson and the specialist, departed from the Studio Tower.

As Louise journeyed through the snow with the others, she brought up a question that had been puzzling her.

"Josy," she said, "the oddest thing happened tonight. Miss Robertson turned on the radio and we heard someone whistling. It sounded exactly like you, yet it couldn't have been because you were on your way to the tower at the time."

"I *was* whistling tonight," confessed Josy. "You didn't hear that over the radio. I was whistling as I came down the path toward the tower."

"But you *were* the performer when we thought we heard you on the radio?" asked Jean shrewdly.

"I have so many things to tell you," replied Josy, "that I really don't know where to begin. But first tell me how you located me."

Quickly Jean explained what had taken place at Starhurst, how they had made a wise guess, and of the letters.

"No one else whistles quite the same as you do, Josy," commented Louise, "so we shouldn't take too much credit."

Josy laughed happily.

"You are too sharp for me. I should have known that the Dana girls would find me out."

"It wasn't hard to guess," said Louise. "We heard your whistle. A radio was working. You weren't anywhere around. Therefore the whistling must have come over the radio."

"Oh, Josy!" cried Jean in excitement. "It's really true! You *are* broadcasting. How exciting that is. Tell us about it."

Josy only smiled mysteriously.

"I'll tell you all my adventures when we reach Barnwold Farm," she promised. "You'll have to be patient."

"Not for long," declared Jean, seizing her by the arm. "For here we are at the front path. Josy Sykes, just as soon as we get into the house I want to hear a full and complete account of your doings."

"And you shall have it," promised Josy, laughing.

Flushed and excited, eager to tell their cousin the good news they were bringing from the

Studio Tower, the girls hurried up onto the veranda and rushed into the picturesque old farmhouse.

"Cousin Bessie!" they called out. "Cousin Bessie!"

A cheery blaze was crackling in the living room fireplace, but the room was deserted. Cousin Bessie had not yet returned from her journey to Majestic. Mrs. Graves, the housekeeper, came in to assure the girls that Miss Marsh expected them to spend the night. She had left word that she would return by the late train from the city.

"In that case," said Louise, drawing chairs up to the fire, "we shall sit up for her."

"I think tea and cinnamon toast should help," beamed Mrs. Graves, bustling off toward the kitchen.

"And now for your story, Josy," said Jean.

# CHAPTER XIX

## An Explanation

"I have really been very lucky," confessed Josy when the girls were comfortably settled before the fire, sipping their tea and sampling a huge platter of fragrant cinnamon toast and other good things from the kitchen. "When I ran away from here, I didn't know where I was going or what I should do. However, I had my thousand-dollar bill and I knew it would keep me for some time."

"But why," asked Jean, "did you run away?"

"I explained that in my note. I felt that I had been the cause of that terrible quarrel between your cousin and Mr. Wheeler, and I thought I was being a burden to you."

"You weren't," Louise assured her warmly.

"Perhaps I am too sensitive. But I have good reason to be. For years I've been pointed at and avoided and scorned by people—because of my misfortune. I realize that I am hideous and deformed and ugly——"

"No!" cried Jean. "You mustn't say such dreadful things."

"But it's true. Ever since I can remember, people have shrunk from me. Can you blame me for being sensitive? I ran away because I wanted to start life all over again with my own money, where I shouldn't be a burden to anyone," Josy declared simply.

"And where did you go?"

"I went to Majestic. You see, I thought that if I were to go to a large city there would be little chance of my being seen and recognized by people whom I knew. When I reached the bus terminal, I asked the policeman on duty to direct me to the Y.W.C.A. I planned to stay there overnight and look for a good lodging house next day. Well," said Josy, "you can imagine my surprise while getting dressed in my room at the Y next morning, to be told that a gentleman was waiting to see me downstairs."

"A gentleman to see you! But you didn't know anyone in Majestic!" cried Louise.

"That's what I thought. I was sure there was some mistake and I said so. But they insisted that the man asked for Miss Josy Sykes, so downstairs I went and found him waiting for me."

"Who was he?"

"Bart Wheeler," replied Josy, calmly.

Her puzzled listeners plied her with questions. How had Bart Wheeler discovered her whereabouts in Majestic? Why had he followed her to the city?

"I couldn't understand it," Josy admitted. "But it was simple enough when he explained. He knew I had taken the bus to Majestic, so when he arrived at the terminal he made inquiries about me. I'm not very hard to trace," she said ruefully. "He learned where I had gone, so there he was in the waiting room when I went downstairs."

"And then—?" asked Jean.

"Mr. Wheeler had called to apologize because he had doubted my word when I claimed the money and the letter. He also wanted to tell me that he had not realized I was crippled, and that he was very sorry to have embarrassed me before my friends. He urged me to go back to Barnwold Farm. However, I told him that I had decided to strike out for myself. Although he tried to persuade me that my course was unwise, I stuck to my decision.

"He told me that he had come to Majestic to do some executive work for the art exhibit, and that he wasn't going back to the Studio Tower because his love affair with Miss Marsh was over. He seemed very downcast and discouraged. However, he said he wanted to help me and suggested that I try the broadcasting stations. He realized that my appearance was against me in most other lines of work, but that my misfortune doesn't matter in that kind of work.

"Then, too, he had been told that I had some talent as a whistler and singer and thought I might be able to get a job on one of the sustaining programs—that is, one of the regular station programs that are on the air whenever a network feature isn't coming through.

"I was delighted at the chance, of course, particularly when Mr. Wheeler told me he was acquainted with the program chief of one of the stations. He said that if I wished him to, he would introduce me to this man and see that I had an audition. I could scarcely credit my good luck. So directly after breakfast I went down to the broadcasting studio with Mr. Wheeler.

"I'll never forget that audition. I was very frightened and nervous, but everyone was kind and I was determined to make good. I knew it was my one big chance, so I whistled as I had never whistled before and sang my very best. When I came out of the studio and went into the program manager's office to learn the result of the audition, I was trembling all over. However, he said the test had been very successful, that I had a good radio voice, and that my whistling was something out of the ordinary.

"It seems that the station had a sustaining

program for which they needed an unusual introduction and he thought my whistling would be just what was wanted. I go on the air several nights a week and help in the office during the daytime, but they are planning a program of my very own."

"I think it's wonderful," said Jean. "Why, you may be famous, Josy. Perhaps you'll be engaged for one of those big programs which pay hundreds of dollars a week."

"I'm quite satisfied. I'm earning enough money to be independent now and that's all that matters. At last," said Josy earnestly, "I'm not a burden to anyone."

The front door opened. Cousin Bessie, looking weary and discouraged, came into the living room, shaking the snow from her wraps. When she saw Josy and the Dana girls, her face lighted up and she hugged them warmly.

Instantly an excited babel of explanations broke forth, in which Miss Melbourne's remarkable recovery, Josy's good fortune and half a dozen other narratives were incoherently mixed. Cousin Bessie clapped her hands over her ears.

"One at a time!" she begged, laughing. "One at a time, please! First of all—how is Constance?"

When they told her of Miss Melbourne's miraculous turn for the better after Josy's visit she was overjoyed. Bit by bit the whole story was unfolded, from the invalid's confession to the dramatic arrival of Josy. It was not, however, until Josy had told the story of her adventures in Majestic that Cousin Bessie explained why she had gone to the city that afternoon.

"I wanted to locate Bart," she said. "When you gave me the address you saw written on the letter to Claude Fayle, I decided to wait no longer. I took the afternoon train immediately after you went over to the Studio Tower."

"Did you find him?" they cried.

An expression of deep discouragement crossed Cousin Bessie's face.

"He had moved. I had my trip for nothing," she answered.

"But didn't he leave a forwarding address?" asked Louise.

"No. His landlady said she didn't know where he had gone."

"He can be traced through the art exhibit," declared Louise promptly.

"I know he has been working very hard to make it a success," said Josy. "Oh, you must find him, Miss Marsh, and fix up your quarrel. He really feels that you don't care for him any more. That is why he has never written to you, I'm sure."

"But I do care for him!" cried Cousin

Bessie. "No one knows how bitterly I have regretted that awful quarrel."

"Would you marry him if he came back?" asked Louise.

"I would indeed—if he were to ask me again. But I hardly think I need go back to Majestic to look for him, for I'm sure he has changed his mind about wanting me for his wife."

"I have an idea," said Jean. "Uncle Ned and Aunt Harriet are going to take us to the art exhibit. Why not come with us? Bart is sure to be at the show. Then you will have an opportunity of seeing him."

"I might do that," agreed Bessie. "I hadn't really planned to go to the exhibit because Constance is not going to be able to show any pictures this season."

"I think she will be showing one—but she won't know about it," Louise remarked.

She went on to explain how Claude Fayle had advanced his reputation in Penfield by his claim that he was to be one of the exhibitors at the forthcoming show. She had a hunch, Louise declared, that Claude Fayle's offering would be none other than the portrait he had stolen from the Studio Tower.

"But he wouldn't dare!" said Bessie hotly.

"Why not? The picture was unsigned. He might easily pass it off as his own work."

The girls then explained to the mystified Josy that the stolen portrait had been painted from a photograph of her uncle when he was a young man. They told her how they had encountered Claude Fayle in Penfield and how they had watched him in an unsuccessful effort to locate the stolen picture. Bessie was particularly indignant when they told of how he was imposing on the wealthy people of Penfield.

"World-famous artist!" she scoffed. "Five thousand dollars for a portrait. I doubt if Claude Fayle ever got as much as five dollars for one of his pictures. You should expose the man."

"No one would believe us," said Louise. "It would make too many people in Penfield look and feel ridiculous. Fayle would brazen it out in some way."

"I suppose he would," sighed Bessie. "That fellow has more nerve than anyone I have ever seen."

They were interrupted by a hearty knock at the door. Bessie leaped up, startled.

"I hope Constance hasn't had a relapse!" she exclaimed, her face pale.

The caller was Miss Melbourne's physician. He had merely dropped in for a moment, he said, to tell them that the patient's condition was showing a decided improvement.

"It is amazing how she has rallied," he said. "Unless there should be a most unexpected setback I have no doubt of her recovery now."

Then he spoke to Josy.

"Will you be able to call and see her tomorrow?" he asked. "It seems to mean a great deal to her, so I promised I would come over and ask you."

"I should be only too glad to call," Josy answered.

The doctor went on his way. The cripple's face shone with happiness. It was a novel experience for her to feel that someone needed her, and that she had brought strength and comfort to another.

"Josy," said Jean, "we have cleared up a great many things that have puzzled us. But there is something else. Please don't think I'm inquisitive——"

"What is it?" asked Josy.

"It's about the letter you were reading when we first met you on the Mohawk Lake trail. It was from your uncle, wasn't it?"

"Yes," replied Josy, "it was from Joseph Sykes. It was my uncle who sent me the thousand-dollar bill."

"But where is he now? If Miss Melbourne could only see him——"

Tears gathered in Josy's eyes.

"I—I am afraid he is dead," she answered slowly.

"Dead! Are you sure?"

"It's the uncertainty of it that is so terrible," replied the girl. "I have no way of knowing. But since that letter, I have had no further word from him, so I fear the worst."

"Perhaps," suggested Bessie gently, "if you care to let us hear the letter we might be able to help you."

Josy got up and went for her handbag. From it she took the letter which she had treasured ever since it had been returned to her by Bart Wheeler.

"I'll be glad to read it to you," she said. "My poor uncle wanted to do so much for me, and he was able to do so little. I have small hope that he is still alive, because otherwise he would try to get in touch with me."

"But he wouldn't know where to find you," Louise pointed out. "A letter may be waiting for you back at the Home for Crippled Children."

"I hadn't thought of that," Josy confessed.

Then she unfolded the worn pages.

# CHAPTER XX

## THE MYSTERY OF JOSEPH SYKES

"THERE are really two letters," explained Josy. "One is from my uncle and the other is from a stranger who found it and mailed it to me. But I'll read my uncle's letter first." She went on as follows:

"MY DEAR JOSY:

"It is many years since you have heard from me. This, I am afraid, must be my farewell to you and to the world, for I am a very sick man and I fear that I have not long to live.

"I am writing this in my little cabin on a remote island in Maine. For years I have cut myself off from the world. I have made my living by trapping and hunting, and although at one time I hoped I should have a considerable fortune to leave you, that hope has been destroyed. However, what little is left must be yours. This letter, in a sense, is my will.

"I came into this wilderness when you were a child. It has been a hard life, but

166

I have had no desire to return to civilization. The world treated me badly, Josy, and when you sustained the terrible injury that deformed you for life, I was nearly insane with grief.

"Perhaps it was unmanly, but I could not bear to see you grow up, knowing how you would suffer when you became old enough to realize that your deformity barred you from the life of normal girls. I made arrangements to have you admitted to the Home at Bonny Lake, and from time to time I sent money for your care.

"I accumulated a considerable fortune by my trapping and by some prospecting above the Canadian border, but two men whom I trusted betrayed my confidence and disappeared with the greater part of my money. This last blow destroyed my faith in humanity, and I have seldom left my little island cabin since then.

"I have been ill for several months. I do not think I shall ever leave this cabin alive. It is little enough I have to leave you, Josy, but several years ago when I had more money than I have now I took a thousand-dollar bill and hid it in a safe place in my cabin, so that I would never be left wholly destitute.

"I shall enclose that bill in this letter.

It is your inheritance. When you receive this message, you will know that I am dead and gone. I am addressing the envelope to you, and if an accident should befall me or if I should be taken ill and be unable to get help, I hope the letter will be found and sent on to you.

"And now, dear Josy, goodbye. I should like to see you once again, but perhaps it is better that I remain out of your life. I fear you have little cause to be grateful to me. For my neglect of you I ask your forgiveness."

Josy looked up.

"That is all," she said.

"Then you don't know whether he is living or not!" cried Louise.

"Another letter was enclosed with his message," Josy told them. "I'll read it now. It is from a hunter who found my uncle in his cabin and who forwarded everything to me."

She read the following:

"DEAR MISS SYKES:

"I am enclosing a letter addressed to you which I found under very strange circumstances a few weeks ago. While on a hunting trip in the Maine woods this autumn, I became separated from my party and was lost for three days. During my wanderings I came upon a cabin on an island. When I entered the place I found a man lying upon the bed. He was evidently seriously ill, so ill that he was unable to talk to me or tell me his name. He seemed anxious that I should take care of the letter which was lying on a table nearby. He continually pointed at it and did not seem happy until I picked it up and promised to look after it.

"As this man may be a near relative, I am informing you of what happened. A searching party found me the following day, and we did what we could for the sick man, bringing him out toward the coast until we reached a monastery. There we left him in the care of the brothers of the order, although I was afraid they would not be able to do much for him. It was my opinion that he had not long to live.

"This monastery is at the little village of Rocky Point. Inasmuch as I've been obliged to return to my home in Boston, I was unable to learn the outcome of his illness.

"Trusting I have been of service to you, I remain,

"Sincerely,
"JAMES B. WENTWORTH."

The letter, written on heavy legal paper, rustled crisply in Josy's hands as she folded it and replaced it in the envelope.

"Did you write to the authorities at the monastery?" asked Louise.

Josy shook her head.

"I took it for granted that my uncle had died," she said. "Just a few days after I got the letter I had to leave the Home—over that trouble about the money—and then the letter was lost, so that I couldn't get the address of the monastery. So I have never inquired."

"He may have recovered," said Jean. "If he is still living, we must find him." Impetuously she went over to Cousin Bessie's writing desk, rummaging about for pen, ink, and writing paper. "I'll write to the monks this very minute. And we'll send the letter by air mail."

Jean's pen sped rapidly across the paper. Louise came over to her side and made suggestions here and there while her impulsive sister was writing. The letter, addressed to Joseph Sykes in care of the monastery at Rocky Point, gave something of Josy's history and expressed her anxiety to learn of her uncle's fate.

"And tell him, please," begged Josy, "that he must come to me. I'll be able to take care of him now—if he is alive."

Josy made no secret of the idea, however, that she believed her uncle to be dead.

When the letter was duly written, read aloud and approved by Josy and Cousin Bessie, the girls planned to see that it was mailed early next morning. It had been a strenuous and exciting day, and when the girls went to bed shortly afterwards, they were so tired that they fell instantly asleep.

"I must go back to Majestic this afternoon," Josy informed them at breakfast next morning. "I'm a working girl now, you know."

"You must see Miss Melbourne before you leave," said Bessie. "I do wish you could stay for a few days, Josy."

"It can't be managed, I'm afraid. There would be dozens of other whistlers looking for my job if I took a holiday without leave," smiled Josy.

"We'll go over to the Studio Tower with you," Jean said. "We want to see Miss Melbourne before we leave."

When the girls called at the Tower that morning, they found Mammy Cleo singing joyously in the kitchen. The old colored servant was bubbling over with happiness as she told the girls that Miss Melbourne had spent a restful night and was rapidly regaining her strength.

"She's gwine get well mighty quick," declared Mammy Cleo. "Jes' go right up de stairs. She's 'spectin' you."

Miss Melbourne greeted them with a brave smile when they entered the sickroom. It was already apparent that she was on the way to recovery. Her eyes were brighter and clearer. There was a faint flush of color in her cheeks.

"It's so good of you to come," she said gratefully. "I was hoping you would call to see me this morning. I have so much to ask you."

"And we have a great deal to tell you," cried Jean gaily.

For the next hour the sickroom echoed with their eager voices. Josy's story was told, the letter of Joseph Sykes was read, and the Dana girls explained how they had written to the monastery at Rocky Point in the hope of learning definitely whether Josy's uncle was still living. Miss Melbourne's thin fingers clutched at the coverlet.

"Oh, I must see him again. I must see him," she murmured.

"We should receive an answer from the monastery in a few days," Louise said.

This was the one flaw that marred Miss Melbourne's delight in her reunion with Josy. If she could only feel sure that Joseph Sykes was alive and well, she said, she would be happy. But mystery enshrouded the fate of the man who had led a solitary existence for so many years.

The doctor arrived for his morning visit and the girls went away. Jean and Louise were thoughtful. Many of the riddles that had confronted them were solved, but there was yet work to do. They must clear Josy's name and absolve her from all suspicion of the theft at the Home for Crippled Children. They must recover Miss Melbourne's portrait. They must locate Bart Wheeler and try to clear up the misunderstanding between him and Cousin Bessie. And they must learn the fate of Joseph Sykes.

"Why should we go back to Starhurst?" said Louise. "The art exhibit in Majestic is to be held on Monday, and we've already made arrangements to go with Uncle Ned and Aunt Harriet. Perhaps if we call Mrs. Crandall, she'll let us go on to Oak Falls. Then we can go back to school with her after the exhibit."

They telephoned to Mrs. Crandall as soon as they returned to Barnwold Farm. The headmistress of Starhurst readily gave her consent.

"Some of the students are going to the art exhibit with me," she said. "We'll meet you there. We are all hoping that Mr. Fayle's picture will win first prize."

Louise did not express her thoughts on the subject of Mr. Fayle.

"Yes," she said, "we're very eager to see the picture he is exhibiting."

When she replaced the receiver, she said to Cousin Bessie:

"Won't you come to Oak Falls with us and go on to the art exhibit from there?"

Miss Marsh shook her head.

"I have been thinking it over," she replied, "and have decided not to go to the art exhibit."

"But why not?" they demanded in astonishment.

"I'm not going to pursue Bart. If he wants to return to me of his own free will, I shall be waiting for him."

The girls were silent. They appreciated their cousin's position, and realized that she would be taking an undignified course in seeking Bart Wheeler. If he refused to return to her, she would be humiliated beyond measure.

"Well, then," said Louise, "we'll just have to see what we can do."

"Yes," Jean declared. "We must see that everything comes out for the best."

# CHAPTER XXI

## THE ACCUSATION

THE art exhibit had been intensively advertised in the city of Majestic as well as throughout the surrounding country. The opening day saw throngs of art lovers flocking to the Municipal Gallery, one of the finest public buildings in the city. Painters from all over the country had entered their productions in the exposition.

Considerable disappointment had been expressed because Miss Constance Melbourne, acknowledged to be one of the foremost portrait painters in America, had been unable to submit an entry. The Jacobsen Medal, one of the great awards in the world of art, was at stake this year and would go to the painter who submitted the finest portrait. Miss Melbourne, although she had won many prizes and honors in her career, had never yet achieved the Jacobsen Medal.

Among the many visitors from out of town who were bound for the exhibit were the Dana girls. Aunt Harriet, who had a sincere appreciation of the artistic, had prevailed upon

Uncle Ned to head the party. Although Captain Dana, hale and hearty, grumbled that he would be out of his element, he came along willingly enough. He was a bluff, jovial seaman of the old school, and was now enjoying a few days' leave while his ship, *The Balaska,* was in port.

When Uncle Ned took a vacation, he took it whole-heartedly. The party registered at the best hotel in Majestic when they arrived on the morning train from Oak Falls.

"We'll stay for two days," he decided. "You ought to be able to stock up on enough art to last you a couple of years, Harriet," at which he winked at the girls. "When you've seen all the pictures, I think it would be a good idea for you to look in a few shop windows. Maybe you'll find some dresses you'd like to get. I have a few dollars in my pocketbook, and if there is anything left over, I'll buy myself a new necktie or a pair of shoe laces."

The art exhibit opened at two o'clock in the afternoon, the judges having spent the morning in viewing the scores of pictures entered in the show. It was announced that some of the major awards would be made public that same day.

"I hope we see Bart Wheeler," said Jean as they ascended the marble steps of the Majestic Art Gallery.

"We'll have an interesting little talk with that young man if we do," declared Louise.

When they entered the main exhibition room and inquired for Wheeler, however, the clerk at the information desk informed them that the object of their search was no longer connected with the art exhibit.

"We were very sorry to lose Mr. Wheeler," he said. "He did a great deal of work for the show and much of its success is due to him. However, a few days ago he said that he did not think he would be needed any more —and away he went."

"Did he leave the city?" asked Louise in disappointment.

"I really couldn't say. I'm afraid I can't give you any help because I happen to know that he left his rooming house last week. Whether or not he is in Majestic now I am unable to tell you."

"And that," said Jean, "is that!"

They turned away from the information desk.

"Any word of him?" asked Uncle Ned, who had been told the whole story.

"He isn't with the art exhibit any more," replied Louise.

"Well, don't let it spoil your day," Uncle Ned advised. "He'll turn up some time, sooner or later."

They began making the rounds of the various rooms and halls. Every inch of space was occupied, for entries had been submitted from all parts of the United States. The success of the show was assured.

Then, above the steady buzz and murmur of the crowd, there arose a shrill, familiar voice.

"My dear, isn't that landscape just too fascinating!"

Jean looked up.

"There isn't another voice like it in the whole world."

"Our dear classmate," said Louise.

"Lettie Briggs!"

Standing before a huge summer landscape they saw several of the girls from Starhurst. Among them were the angular Lettie and her chum, Ina Mason.

"The color is so intriguing!" gushed Lettie. "And the chiaroscuro! Masterly! Simply divine!"

The other girls looked at Lettie with great respect. None of them knew what chiaroscuro was, and few of them could pronounce it.

"I do wish my portrait had been finished in time," went on Lettie, in a voice meant to reach those standing nearby. "Mr. Fayle said he would enter it in this exhibit if he could get it ready. It's being painted by Mr. Claude Fayle, you know. He has another portrait on exhibition here today and they say it may win the Jacobsen Medal.''

One of the other girls immediately expressed a desire to see Claude Fayle's masterpiece, and Lettie proudly led them toward a small room off the main hall. The Dana girls, who were also curious, promptly followed.

"Isn't it wonderful!" Lettie said, indicating a beautifully framed and skillfully lighted portrait which hung in solitary grandeur on the wall. "He says it's the finest piece of work he has ever done. But really—if *my* portrait had been finished in time——''

The rest of Lettie's gushing praise was lost on the Dana girls. They were gazing spellbound at the portrait.

*It was the painting that had been stolen from the Studio Tower!*

There it was, just as they remembered it—the portrait of Joseph Sykes. There was one difference now, however. In the lower right-hand corner the girls could distinguish the bold signature of Claude Fayle.

They were amazed at the impudence of his deception. Much to their sorrow, they now realized that his trickery had every chance of success. Miss Melbourne would not be at the exhibit to claim the portrait as her own. She had kept the picture draped while it was in her studio, and few people had ever been privileged to view it. She had not signed her name to it, and to all intents and purposes the portrait now belonged to Claude Fayle and was accepted as his own work.

"I know what we'll do," said Louise quickly. "We'll see the committee of judges about this. That portrait is perfect enough to win the medal—and why shouldn't it? Miss Melbourne's work! But Claude Fayle isn't going to get the credit if we can help it."

They left the room and struggled through the crowd, trying to reach the administration office of the art show. They had not gone far before they saw a stout, flabby young man in a broad-brimmed hat and Windsor tie making his way in lordly fashion across the hall. He was surrounded by a little group of admirers and the effect was that of a triumphant procession.

"Claude Fayle himself!" exclaimed Jean.

"Shall we speak to him now?"

"Why not?"

This was easier said than done. Claude Fayle was receiving the homage of a little group of people who had heard the rumor that he was almost certain to be the winner of the medal. The girls found it difficult to make their way to his side. A moment later Lettie Briggs and Ina Mason spied him and descended upon him headlong.

"Oh, Mr. Fayle!" squealed Lettie, elbowing various innocent bystanders as she fought her way toward the hero of the hour. "I'm so glad you've come. We have just been admiring your portrait. It's simply marvellous. There isn't anything else like it in the entire show!"

"Thank you. Thank you," murmured Claude Fayle, beaming.

Lettie, eager to impress all within hearing, rattled on.

"I do hope you'll soon be able to get back at my portrait, Mr. Fayle. I'm afraid you'll have so many orders now that you won't have time for poor little me."

"I shall always have time for you, Miss Briggs," replied Fayle gallantly.

"And why not—for five thousand dollars?" murmured Jean.

"If she can get through this crowd and speak to him, then so can we," declared Louise emphatically.

They thrust their way through the throng, and by dint of much pushing and shoving managed to range themselves beside Lettie and Ina.

"How do you do, Mr. Fayle?" said Louise pleasantly.

Claude Fayle glanced at her, recognized her, and then frowned. Lettie tossed the Dana girls a contemptuous look.

"Oh, Mr. Fayle!" she exclaimed. "Won't

you come with me and look at the portrait?
I am so eager to have you tell me in your own
words just how you managed such a *marvellous*
color effect.''

"Gladly!" agreed Claude Fayle, who seemed
eager to escape. "I'll go with you now."

Lettie smiled maliciously at the Dana girls.

"I'm afraid Claude is too busy to talk to
you just now," she said.

Jean ignored her.

"While you are explaining the portrait to
Lettie," the younger Dana said to Claude
Fayle, "perhaps you had better tell her who
painted it."

The artist flushed.

"What's that?" he said. "What do you
mean?"

"We mean," said Louise flatly, "that you
didn't paint that picture!"

There were instant protestations from Lettie
and Ina, followed by a splutter of rage from
Claude Fayle. But the Dana girls were un-
moved.

"That picture was painted by Constance
Melbourne. You stole it from her studio.
You are exhibiting her work as your own,"
declared Jean.

Claude Fayle recovered his composure.

"I don't know what you are talking about,"
he said calmly. "The portrait is my own

work. If you don't believe me, go look at the
signature. If Miss Melbourne painted it, why
didn't she sign her name to it? I took it from
her studio because I had left it there for safe-
keeping. Now, if you will stop annoying me
by your silly and idiotic accusations, I'll be on
my way.''

The girls were so astounded by Claude
Fayle's cool denial that they could think of
nothing to say. In another moment the artist
had shouldered his way past them.

"Why, the very idea!" exclaimed Lettie
Briggs, and with a withering glance at the
Dana girls she followed her hero.

The incident had caused a stir among the
crowd, and when Claude Fayle sauntered
calmly on his way and left the Dana girls standing speechless, several people snickered. Jean
and Louise flushed with embarrassment.
Claude Fayle had won a momentary victory and
had made them look decidedly foolish.

"I guess you won't be so free with your
smart remarks after this," snapped an old
lady who had been standing within earshot.

Just then a burly figure emerged from the
crowd. It was Uncle Ned.

"What's the trouble?" he asked quietly.

The girls told him. Uncle Ned frowned.

"You gave him his chance," said Captain
Dana. "He thinks he can bluff you. Better

tell the president of the Art Society. Here he comes now.''

He indicated a dignified, white-haired man just emerging from a nearby office, followed by a number of committee members of the exhibit.

''They're on their way to announce the prize awards,'' said Uncle Ned. ''Don't waste any time.''

Louise and Jean quickly stepped over and confronted the elderly gentleman, who was scanning a sheaf of papers.

''I beg your pardon, Sir—'' ventured Jean.

The president looked up.

''I'm sorry,'' he said. ''I haven't time to talk to anyone now. We're just going to announce the prize winners.''

''But it's about Claude Fayle!'' exclaimed Louise desperately.

''Mr. Fayle? Is he a friend of yours? You may be glad to know that he has been awarded the Jacobsen Medal for the remarkable portrait he has exhibited here.''

''But he doesn't deserve the medal! He didn't paint that picture!'' Jean cried.

## CHAPTER XXII

### Justice Is Done

Her accusation amazed the president.

"Are you serious?" he exclaimed.

"We are," cried Louise. "Claude Fayle did not paint that portrait, and we can prove it."

"Please come with me," said the president, turning abruptly and leading the way to his office. "This situation must be investigated."

He spoke quietly to the astonished members of the committee on awards, who returned at once to the executive room.

"These young ladies," explained the president, "have just made a very serious charge against one of the artists exhibiting here to-day. They claim that the portrait for which we have been about to award Mr. Claude Fayle the Jacobsen Medal was not, in fact, painted by Mr. Fayle at all."

There was a low murmur of amazement and consternation.

"I think," spoke up one of the members of the committee, "that Mr. Fayle should have an opportunity to defend himself. He should be here."

The others agreed that this was a proper course, in view of the serious nature of the charge. Claude Fayle was summoned to the office. In a few minutes he entered, a defiant smirk upon his face as he confronted the stern, serious men.

"Now then, young ladies," said the president curtly. "Please tell us what you have to say."

"We have this to say," replied Louise bravely. "The portrait which Mr. Fayle exhibited here today as his own was never painted by him. He has signed his name to it, but the picture is not his work."

"This is outrageous!" blustered Claude Fayle. "Gentlemen, must I defend myself against such a ridiculous charge? The portrait is my own work!"

"If it was not painted by Mr. Fayle," said the president, "then who did paint it?"

"Miss Constance Melbourne!" exclaimed Jean.

"But if Miss Melbourne painted the picture, she would have signed her name to it!" said one of the committee members. "The signature is that of Mr. Fayle."

"Exactly!" said Claude Fayle. "These girls have some ridiculous notion that I stole the portrait from Miss Melbourne's studio. They have already publicly accused me of the theft. I explained that I had left the portrait in the studio for safe-keeping. Miss Melbourne, I might say, is a very dear friend of mine. She happened to be ill when I called for the picture, and these girls thought they saw me taking away something which did not belong to me. I brought the portrait to my studio in Penfield, finished it, signed it, and placed it on exhibition here. That is all there is to the affair.''

His glib story created an impression.

''Haven't you made a mistake?'' asked the president of Louise.

''Not at all. Mr. Fayle is not telling the truth. The portrait was painted by Miss Melbourne. She told us so. She does not know it was taken from her studio. Miss Melbourne has worked at the picture for years.''

Louise went on to explain the circumstances under which they had first seen the picture, and told how they had seen Claude Fayle steal out of the Studio Tower with a bulky object beneath his cloak.

The artist stubbornly denied the charge. He blustered and stormed, threatened to remove the portrait from the exhibition, and brazenly declared that the girls were lying.

''Who is the subject of the picture?'' asked Jean shrewdly.

Claude Fayle hesitated for a moment.

"It was a professional model," he said.
"His name?"

"I—I forget."

Jean turned to the committee.

"The portrait was painted from a photograph and from memory. The name of the man was Joseph Sykes, an old friend of Miss Melbourne."

The president of the Art Society was convinced by now that the Dana girls were telling the truth. Their story had been clearly told, with details that could not have been invented. Besides, he reflected, there was no reason why they should invent such a tale and every reason in the world why Claude Fayle should deny it.

The other men in the room were apparently of the same opinion, because they began questioning the artist. When had he commenced work on the picture? When had it been completed? Where did he employ the model? Why had he left the portrait at Miss Melbourne's studio, as he claimed? Question after question was hurled at the panic-stricken artist. He became confused, contradicted himself, and floundered miserably.

"The picture is mine!" he shouted. "I painted it."

But the members of the committee had been convinced. They sent for the painting. Its workmanship was compared to that of an authentic portrait known to have been painted by Constance Melbourne.

Claude Fayle was next questioned about his previous career. He made absurd claims which were quickly shown to be false after the officials had looked up records on file in the office. At last, realizing that he was trapped, he broke down and made a complete confession.

"Let me go!" he begged. "Don't have me arrested. I stole the portrait and tried to pass it off as my own work."

The president's face was stern. He pointed toward the door.

"Get out!" he snapped. "If you aren't out of this building within two minutes, I'll have you arrested."

Claude Fayle made a hasty and ignominious retreat. He scuttled out of the room, fled from the art gallery, and presumably lost no time in leaving the city. The Dana girls never heard of him again, and it is certain that he did not return to Penfield to finish the five-thousand-dollar portrait of Lettie Briggs.

Jean and Louise were warmly congratulated by the committee of judges. A great injustice had been narrowly averted, and a gross impostor had been unmasked.

"The Jacobsen Medal," said the president quietly, "will go, of course, to Miss Melbourne.

The portrait was not entered in her name, but that's a mere formality that can be straightened out. The award is for the picture, not for the name."

Thus it happened, that when the committee later made its long-awaited announcement to the audience, the crowd was stunned by the news that the coveted medal had been awarded to Miss Constance Melbourne.

"Due to the efforts of two clever girls who kept their eyes open and were courageous enough to speak up at the right time," said the president, "we have learned that the prize-winning picture was being exhibited here by an impostor. Fortunately he has been exposed as a rascal, and we are glad to know that Miss Melbourne—without her own knowledge or intention—contributed a masterpiece to our exhibition after all."

Uncle Ned and Aunt Harriet were proud and delighted. It became rumored about that the Dana girls had been responsible for the discovery of the truth which had brought about Claude Fayle's downfall. People sought introductions, asked eager questions, and wanted to know all the details of the affair. Mrs. Crandall, headmistress of Starhurst, beamed with delight and let it be known that the girls were students of her school.

"They have a decided talent for detective

work," said the headmistress. "The Dana girls have solved several important cases to my knowledge."

Lettie Briggs was nowhere to be found. She did not care to be reminded of the five-thousand-dollar portrait.

The Dana girls asked one favor of the committee before they returned to their hotel.

"May we have the portrait?" asked Louise. "Miss Melbourne has been very ill. She didn't intend to exhibit the painting, and we know she prefers to have it near her in her studio. Then too, we want to show it to a friend of ours—a girl to whom it will mean a great deal."

Their request was granted. When Uncle Ned saw them carrying the portrait down the marble steps, he declared that the occasion justified calling a taxi.

"It isn't every day in the week," he said, "that we go to an art exhibit and come home with a first-prize picture."

When the girls returned to the hotel, they telephoned to the office of the broadcasting station where Josy Sykes was employed. As the voice of the crippled girl came over the wire, Louise cried:

"Josy! Can you come up to see us right away?"

"Of course. But where are you?"

They told her the name of the hotel and gave their room number.

"We have something to show you," said Jean. "Please hurry! It's important!"

Josy Sykes arrived in less than half an hour. The Dana girls, in the meantime, had propped the portrait up on a chair so that the light shone on it and brought out the perfection of its coloring and workmanship.

When Josy arrived a little later and saw the handsome features of the young man smiling at her from the canvas, she uttered a little gasp and then looked up inquiringly at the girls.

"Is it—my uncle?" she faltered.

"We have found the missing portrait," Louise told her.

Josy advanced toward the picture and surveyed it for a long time. Gently she extended her frail hand and touched the canvas. For the first time in her life she was gazing on the likeness of her one and only relative. It meant much to her.

"I was so small when I last saw him," she whispered, "that I have no recollection of him at all."

Josy was curious as to how the girls had recovered the picture. Jean and Louise told her of their adventure at the art gallery, and explained how they had confronted Claude Fayle and forced him to confess. While the story was being told Josy could scarcely take her eyes off the portrait.

"Oh, if he were only alive and well!" she exclaimed. "It would make me so happy."

"We'll hope for the best," said Jean cheerfully. "I can hardly wait for the answer to our letter."

But there was such good humor, courage, and faith in the eyes of the painted Joseph Sykes as he smiled gaily at them from the canvas, that they could not feel discouraged. So great had been the genius of Miss Melbourne that he seemed like a living presence in the room, silently bidding them to be patient and cheerful.

# CHAPTER XXIII

## At the Studio

"WE MUST find Bart Wheeler while we are
waiting for the answer to our letter," declared
Jean. "We can never settle down to study another lesson at Starhurst until we locate him."

"I'm sure he is still in the city," Louise said.

Uncle Ned took a sip of coffee. They were
at breakfast in the hotel the morning after the
art exhibit.

"How are you going to find him?" asked
Uncle Ned.

"We'll simply have to do a little private
detecting."

Aunt Harriet was impressed by Jean's airy
manner.

"I'm sure I shouldn't know how to go about
it. Too much like looking for a needle in a
haystack, trying to find one young man in a
city of this size."

"There are ways and means," remarked
Louise. "He is an artist so is probably in
touch with others of his kind in Majestic. If
we check up carefully, we may find someone
who can tell us where he went."

"Go ahead and look for him, then," said
Uncle Ned. "Your aunt and I are going to
take a day off and go shopping, then enjoy a
movie. We'll have a real good time."

"It does sound rather reckless," smiled
Aunt Harriet.

"We'll go about our detective work while
you're out enjoying the day," Jean laughed.
"Come on, Lou. We'd better get busy."

Before setting out on their search for Bart
Wheeler, the Dana girls outlined a systematic
plan. They realized that haphazard methods
would be useless.

First of all, they called up an official at the
art gallery and asked for the names of some of
the leading artists in the city. From him, too,
they learned who were some of Bart Wheeler's
friends while he had been engaged in his work
on behalf of the exhibit. Finally, with a sub-
stantial list of addresses in their possession,
they set out.

Progress, however, was slow and discourag-
ing. Visit after visit yielded no clue. Not one
of Bart Wheeler's friends knew where he had
gone after finishing his work at the art gallery.
Some said he had talked of leaving the city.
No one had received word from him. He had
dropped out of sight like a stone in a pool.

At the end of the afternoon they were tired
and ready to give up.

"At last," said Jean ruefully, "I think we have found one mystery that stumps us. I don't believe he is in Majestic at all."

Louise was disconsolate.

"I hate to give up. But it does seem as if he dropped out of sight deliberately."

"We'll try these last two addresses. If they fail us I'm afraid we'll have to admit we're beaten."

They called on the two remaining artists on their list. One of them, a man who said he had known Bart Wheeler intimately, was positive that Wheeler had gone away from Majestic.

"If he is still in the city, he would get in touch with me. But he was a peculiar sort of chap—seemed to have something on his mind."

"He did," said Louise.

"Whatever it was, it worried him a great deal. Moody fellow. I'm sorry I can't help you locate him."

The other artist was also unable to give them any assistance, but promised to make inquiries among his friends.

"I'll let you know if I find any trace of him," he promised, and with that the Dana girls had to be content.

Dispirited and weary, they made their way toward the broadcasting station where Josy was employed. They had promised to call for her there. Josy had hinted that she would try to secure passes to one of the studios where they could witness an actual broadcast.

"Have you had any word from the monastery?" Josy asked eagerly when she met them in the outer office of the station.

"None yet," replied Louise in a discouraged tone. "I'm afraid there hasn't been time."

"Did you find Bart Wheeler?"

"No such luck," said Jean. "We've worn out our shoes and our patience today, but still we're up against a blank wall. When do you go on the air, Josy?"

"My program is scheduled for seven forty-five. But there's a dramatic sketch in Studio B within a few minutes. Would you care to watch? The director said I might bring you in with me."

"It would be fun!" they agreed enthusiastically.

Josy led the way through a cozy reception room, beautifully furnished, where several people were waiting. A man whom they presumed to be one of the entertainers was absorbed in a manuscript.

They passed through the reception room and went down a corridor. Through a window they caught a glimpse of a chamber filled with impressive and mystifying machinery. A young man was sitting at a panel. This was the control room, Josy explained, and the youth was one of the most important personages in the studio.

"We must keep perfectly quiet while the sketch is on the air," warned Josy, as she opened the door that admitted them to Studio B to witness the broadcast.

It was a large room, the walls of which were covered with heavy drapes from ceiling to floor. Their shoes sank noiselessly into a deep rug. Half a dozen young men in shirt sleeves, an old man with white hair and a shaggy beard, three pleasant looking girls, and a brusque young fellow who appeared to be trying to do half a dozen things at once, were in the studio.

A cylindrical microphone hung by a wire from the ceiling, and two others were in evidence above a couple of small tables partly surrounded by heavy hangings of felt. In a corner were several odd-looking pieces of apparatus for creating sound effects.

The brusque young man nodded to Josy and gestured toward a row of chairs at the back of the studio.

"We're going on in a minute," he said. He whipped a manuscript from his pocket and turned to the others. "Places!" he said sharply, and looked up at a clock above the door.

The actors took their places. One of the

girls and three of the men sat down at a small
table. The others were seated at the next
microphone. As the bearded actor moved toward his chair the director inquired:

"What's the idea of the make-up?"

"I can do my part better."

The director nodded. A door opened and a
tall man came in, glancing at his wrist watch.
He stepped over to the microphone in the
middle of the room. A boy seated near the
window of the control chamber raised his
hand and brought it down sharply as a red
light glowed.

The announcer spoke quietly and confidently
into the microphone.

"Tonight," he said, "the Studio Players will
offer for your entertainment a dramatic sketch
entitled 'Out of the Storm.' This is the third
in a series of weekly plays presented over this
network Tuesday evenings at this time. The
scene is laid on the Florida coast. A terrific
gale has been raging for two days——"

He spoke on, reading from his manuscript.
After a while he stepped away from the microphone. One of the actors performed some
strange antics with a sheet of tin and a small
box of dried peas. The microphone transformed these into a realistic imitation of the
booming of the surf and the splashing of waves.
The director gestured sharply toward one of

the tables. The actor in the white beard spoke:

"There is no hope, Mary. The ship is lost. She could never live through that storm."

"But Jed is no common sailor, Father," said one of the girls, reading from a sheet of manuscript pasted on cardboard so that it would not rustle when put to one side.

"Aye! But 'twould take an uncommon good man to bring any vessel through such a gale."

The Dana girls listened, enthralled by this glimpse behind the scenes. Away out in the night scores of people were listening to these voices, building up in their minds a picture of a wave-wracked coast, and picturing an old mariner and his daughter standing on the beach, gazing hopelessly out to sea.

Jean sat forward in her chair, her eyes fixed on the bearded actor. She listened intently to every line he spoke. A strange feeling of excitement took possession of her. Half an hour later when the sketch had come to an end, and a light flashed to indicate that Studio B was now "off the air," she turned to Louise.

"The man in the beard!" she whispered. "Did his voice sound familiar to you?"

"Did you notice it too?" exclaimed Louise. "Who do you think it is?"

"Bart Wheeler!"

They quickly arose, and greatly to Josy's

surprise hurriedly crossed the studio in pursuit of the actor. He was halfway down the corridor on the way to his dressing room when they overtook him.

"Mr. Wheeler!" said Jean.

The actor turned and unconsciously revealed his identity.

"Yes?" he answered.

"Then you *are* Bart Wheeler!" cried Louise, joyfully.

He looked at them ruefully. They saw that the white mop of hair was a wig, and that the gray beard masked a young and handsome face.

"Yes," he said with a shrug. "And you are the Dana girls. I remember you well now."

"We've searched all over the city for you," said Jean. "You must come back to Barnwold Farm with us. Please!"

Wheeler laughed bitterly.

"I hope I may never see Barnwold Farm or the Studio Tower again."

"But why?"

"That," returned Bart Wheeler, "is my own affair."

"Don't you know that Miss Melbourne has been dreadfully ill? Don't you know that Bessie has been heartbroken ever since you went away?"

"I don't believe it," said Bart flatly. "She

broke our engagement. She sent me away. So I'm not going back."

"Please sit down, Mr. Wheeler," said Louise, indicating a bench in the corridor. "We want to tell you what has been happening since you left the Studio Tower."

It was a long story, but the Dana girls left nothing untold. As they related the tale of Constance Melbourne's fight for life and of Bessie's vain search for her lover, Bart Wheeler's face grew amazed, then serious.

"This is true?" he said at last. "She really wants me to come back?"

"Why should we have been searching for you," said Jean, "if not for Bessie's sake?"

Bart Wheeler was silent for a moment. He covered his face with his hands.

"I have been a fool!" he groaned. "I really thought she never wanted to see me again. I've been wretched and miserable ever since I came to Majestic. I did what I could to make amends to the little crippled girl. She didn't know I was on the program tonight, or I suppose she would have told you."

"Then," said Louise gently, "you'll come back to Barnwold Farm with us?"

"Yes, I'll come back. If Bessie wants me, I'll come back."

"She does want you," Jean assured him.

At that moment a weird, familiar whistle

sounded through the corridor. Clear and
sweet, it penetrated every corner of the studio.
When the oddly thrilling notes had died away
a girl's voice broke into song.

Josy Sykes was on the air!

The girls listened spellbound as the cripple
sang her opening number. When the last
verse was ended, the intriguing whistle that
was to make Josy's name familiar to thousands
of radio listeners throughout the country
again floated from the radio in the reception
room.

"She has a great talent," said Bart Wheeler.
"Everyone in the studio believes she has a
wonderful future."

The Dana girls were filled with happiness.
Josy Sykes had come into her own at last. If
only her uncle could return to her, the hunchback would be superbly happy.

# CHAPTER XXIV

## The Letter

Two days later the Dana girls said goodbye to Uncle Ned and Aunt Harriet and set out for Barnwold Farm.

"It will be a real home-coming this time," said Jean.

They were returning with Bart Wheeler and Josy Sykes—the one eager to make up his quarrel with Cousin Bessie, the other bubbling over with happiness because of her great success.

Josy's first complete program had brought a flood of letters and telegrams to the studio. She was, in the language of radio, "a find," and had already received flattering offers from the large networks and advertising agencies to go on a coast-to-coast hook-up at a handsome salary.

Only two things were needed to complete her happiness.

"If I could only have Uncle Joseph with me!" she said. "And if I could only clear up that dreadful charge against me of stealing the benefit receipts at the Home."

204

"There should be a letter from the monastery almost any day now," declared Louise. "As for that affair at Bonny Lake—well, we've been thinking of that. Perhaps a little detective work wouldn't be amiss there."

Before they left Majestic the girls told Uncle Ned about the expected letter.

"If it arrives here you must let us know at once," they said. "It may contain bad news, but anything is better than this suspense."

"I'll 'phone you if the message comes," promised Uncle Ned.

It was an altered Josy Sykes who descended from the train at Mount Pleasant. With the help of the Dana girls she had done some shopping before leaving Majestic. New dresses had been chosen so that her deformity was scarcely noticeable. Happiness and good fortune had erased the pitiful lines from her face, and her natural attractiveness had been given a chance to assert itself. Josy, from a poor, frightened, homely little waif, had been transformed into a confident, self-reliant girl, beautifully attired, and with a certain quaint, shy prettiness.

Bart Wheeler, too, was again his old self. Sullen and embittered when he had believed himself discarded by Bessie, he was now blythe and gay, eager with anticipation as they drew closer to Barnwold Farm.

They had not sent word of their coming, so

they took Bessie completely by surprise. When she saw the happy group on the threshold, she uttered a cry of amazement and joy.

"Bart!" she gasped. Then a deep flush suffused her face. "You've come back?"

"Do you want me back, Bessie?"

The expression in her eyes was answer enough. Bart Wheeler strode across the threshold and took her in his arms.

"I think," said Jean tactfully, "we had better go out into the living room. You and Bart will have a lot of things to talk about."

Leaving the reunited pair to themselves, the Dana girls and Josy went out into the big living room where Jean at once began to unpack a cumbersome parcel that had not left her possession since they set out for Barnwold Farm.

It was the portrait of Joseph Sykes.

"We must take this over to the Studio Tower right away," she said.

Just then the telephone rang.

"Take the message, Lou," said Jean. "If anyone asks for Bessie——"

"I'll tell him she is engaged," laughed Louise.

But the message was not for her. It was from Captain Ned Dana, back in the hotel at Majestic.

"Hello, Louise," he said gruffly. "A letter

came for you half an hour after you left the hotel.''

"Is it—from the monastery?" cried Louise.

Jean dropped the wrapping paper from the portrait. Josy Sykes rose to her feet, her eyes wide with suspense.

"I don't know," said Uncle Ned. "I didn't open it. I don't open other people's mail. But the postmark reads Rocky Point."

"Open it, Uncle Ned. Please. Open it at once. Oh, hurry."

"Now, now," said Captain Dana. "Take it easy. The letter won't fly away. Just a minute now." They heard him grumbling to himself. "Where are my specs? I can never find them when I want them. Harriet, where are my specs?"

Louise heard her aunt's voice sweetly saying:

"You pushed them up onto your forehead."

Uncle Ned grunted.

"Humph! Here they are. Now, where's that letter? Where *is* that letter? Here it is, right in my hand." Louise heard him tear open the envelope. "All set?" he asked.

"Yes, Uncle Ned. Please read it to me."

Jean and Josy crowded around the receiver, trying to overhear Uncle Ned's voice.

"Well, it says here that they got your letter."

"Yes, yes. Of course they got our letter.

They wouldn't answer it if they hadn't," cried Louise impatiently.

"That's true," muttered Uncle Ned. "Well, anyway, they say they got your letter and that they're glad to be able to help you."

"But what do they *say?* What has happened to Mr. Sykes?"

"I'm just coming to that," said Uncle Ned with dignity. "If you'll just try to be a little more patient and keep from interrupting me every two minutes——"

Louise sighed.

"Yes, Uncle Ned," she said meekly. "Please go on."

"Well, they say that Joseph Sykes isn't at the monastery."

"But is he living?"

"Oh, he's *alive!*" declared Uncle Ned.

"Thank goodness," breathed Josy Sykes.

"At least," amended Uncle Ned, "I think he must be alive, because he wasn't dead when he left the monastery. It seems they kept him there until he got better. Then he went away."

"But where did he go?"

There was silence for a moment. Uncle Ned was apparently reading the letter through to the end.

"It doesn't say. He didn't tell them where he was going."

"And is that all?" asked Louise, disappointed.

"That's all. I'll send it on to you in the next mail so you can read it yourselves."

Uncle Ned rang off. Louise replaced the receiver and turned to the others. Briefly she told them the import of the letter.

"He is alive and well, at any rate," said Josy. "It's a great comfort to know that. He may have gone back to his cabin on the island."

"Another case for the Dana girls," Louise declared cheerfully. "We'll find him, Josy, wherever he is."

"I don't know how you're going to begin."

"We'll think of something," Jean assured her. "In the meantime we had better bring this portrait back to Miss Melbourne."

When they reached the Studio Tower a few minutes later, Mammy Cleo received them with a shout of welcome; and when the old servant saw the portrait, her joy knew no bounds.

"Good luck come back! Good luck come back agin!" she chanted. "Bad luck come when dat pitcher done got stole. Now ebberyting gwine be all right."

She beamed and chuckled as she gazed at the portrait. Then she put it back carefully in its old place on the easel in the studio.

"Nobody's gwine take dat away frum dis

place no mo'," she declared. "Anybody dat tries it'll git a taste of mah rollin' pin!"

Before they went upstairs to see Miss Melbourne, the Dana girls spoke to Josy.

"Would the manager of your broadcasting station do you a favor, Josy?" asked Louise.

"I'm sure he would."

"I've been thinking of a plan. It may work, and then it may not, but there is no harm in trying. Why can't we try to locate your uncle by radio?"

Josy was puzzled.

"How can we?"

They explained their plan. At first Josy was dubious, but as Louise went into detail she became enthusiastic. Inside of a few minutes she was in touch with the radio station by telephone and had readily obtained the manager's consent to her request. Louise then spoke to him in her businesslike way.

"This is the message we should like to have you broadcast," she said. "Will you copy it down, please? 'Will Joseph Sykes, who recently left the monastery at Rocky Point, please return to his old farm home at Dalton? An important message is awaiting him.'"

"Is that all?"

"That is all, thank you."

"I'll be very glad to have that put on the air tonight," the manager assured her. "As a matter of fact, I'll try to have it broadcast several times.''

"That will be very good of you. I hope it isn't too much trouble.''

"No trouble at all, Miss Dana.''

"And if *that* doesn't bring results,'' Louise declared as they went upstairs, "then radio isn't the marvellous invention I think it is.''

Miss Melbourne's delight when they entered the sickroom was touching. She had made great progress toward recovery since they had last visited her, and greeted them with a cry of joy. Josy ran to her and they clung to each other affectionately.

"We brought back your portrait—and you won the medal—and we found Bart Wheeler— and my program was a big success—and Claude Fayle signed his name to your picture —oh, I have *so* much to tell you!'' declared Josy tumultuously.

Miss Melbourne laughed happily.

"Please don't try to tell it all at once, Josy,'' she begged. "Sit down, girls. You're going to have a nice long visit with me and tell me all the news.''

But the Dana girls glanced at each other.

"I'm afraid we can't stay, Miss Melbourne,'' said Jean. "If you don't mind, we'll leave Josy to tell you all about everything. We're going to be rather busy for a while.''

"But where are you going?" asked Josy in surprise.

"Business," said Jean.

"What sort of business?"

"Detective business."

With this laconic and mysterious announcement the Dana girls vanished from the room.

# CHAPTER XXV

## THE REUNION

"I DO hope nothing has happened to them," said Bessie Marsh anxiously.

Bart Wheeler frowned.

"I'm getting worried," he confessed.

"They should have been back hours ago!" Miss Melbourne exclaimed.

Josy Sykes went over to the window and pressed her face to the pane.

"They didn't say where they were going. But it's dreadfully late now. It's after eleven o'clock. Oh, I hope no harm has come to them."

The Dana girls were missing!

From the moment they had left the Studio Tower late that afternoon there had been no word from them. Now, late at night, the little group in Miss Melbourne's room waited anxiously for their return.

"Do you think," faltered Josy, "that Claude Fayle——?"

"May have tried to get revenge on them?" said Bart. "I was thinking of that. He's an ill-natured rascal."

"It isn't like them to stay out so late without sending word," Bessie said. "I'll never forgive myself if anything has happened to them after all they have done for us."

Josy gazed out over the snow-covered countryside. There was a full moon in the sky, and strange shadows fell across the courtyard beneath the Studio Tower. It was a sinister scene. In the distance a dog howled mournfully. The dreary sound echoed across the lonely countryside.

Josy trembled. She was filled with anxiety for the safety of the two friends who meant so much to her. The mournful howl of the dog sent a chill through her. Was the animal baying at the moon—or something else?

Down in the shadow of the Tower she saw a movement. Someone was crossing the courtyard in the deep gloom below. Josy watched in an agony of suspense.

Then, out of the dark patch of shadow there emerged three figures—two girls and a man. The moonlight shone upon their happy faces.

"They're here!" cried Josy. "I just saw them in the shadow of the tower. And—and —they've brought Uncle Joseph with them."

Bart Wheeler and Bessie ran to the window. Constance Melbourne seemed almost stunned, then raised herself and murmured:

"They've brought Joseph with them?"

"Oh, I'm sure. It must be my uncle," said Josy in excitement.

She was right. A few moments later the Dana girls ascended the winding stairs of the Studio Tower, to be met by an excited group on the landing. With them was a gray-haired, athletic figure whose face bore a startling resemblance to the portrait of Joseph Sykes.

He was, indeed, Josy's long-lost uncle. A vigorous, active man in his early fifties, tanned and bronzed by years of life in the wilds, he came up the stairs arm in arm with the Dana girls. And then tumult broke forth.

Everybody tried to speak at once. Josy fled to the arms of her uncle. Cousin Bessie and Bart Wheeler demanded explanations. Uncle Joseph was introduced all around, and there was so much laughter and chatter and excitement that Mammy Cleo came running wildly from the kitchen, to stand at the foot of the staircase and add her bewildered cries to the general uproar. It was the gladdest, maddest scene that had ever taken place within the walls of the Studio Tower.

"The Dana girls found me," explained Uncle Joseph, as he sat by Constance Melbourne's bedside and clasped her frail hand in his strong brown fingers, "at the old farm in Dalton. I have been living near there, and tonight I heard a radio message urging me to go to the farm. So I did. And these girls were waiting for me."

"Radio," declared Louise solemnly, "is a marvellous invention."

"I had been trying to locate Josy," he said, "but without success. Thanks to the cleverness of these two girls, however, I am here."

This clever sleuthing on the part of the sisters was to be demonstrated again when the opportunity was to be offered to them to solve "A Three-Cornered Mystery."

Gazing fondly at Miss Melbourne, Mr. Sykes whispered, "I am happier now than I have ever been before."

"Your wanderings, Joseph Sykes, are over," said Miss Melbourne firmly.

"And that isn't all!" cried Jean. "We stopped in at the Home for Crippled Children at Bonny Lake on our way back. Josy, we have good news for you."

"About—about the money?" she asked.

"You have been exonerated. The real thief has confessed."

"Miss Robertson was right," said Louise. "The thief was Mrs. Rye."

"So that," remarked Jean, "clears up the last remaining mystery of this whole series of mysteries. The portrait is back in its proper place, Josy has found her uncle——"

"And I have found Constance," interrupted Joseph Sykes.

"And Bart and Bessie are engaged again——"

"So there is nothing left for us now," concluded Louise, "but to go back to Starhurst."

"After all this excitement, you'll be ready to settle down to some hard studying," added Josy.

"Until we find another mystery to solve," said Jean wisely.